P9-AFL-517

DATE DUE

California Suite

CALIFORNIA SUITE

A NEW COMEDY BY

Neil Simon

RANDOM HOUSE · NEW YORK

For Mildred

CALIFORNIA SUITE *was first presented on June 10, 1976, by
Emanuel Azenberg and Robert Fryer at the Eugene O'Neill
Theatre, New York City, with the following cast:*

VISITOR from NEW YORK
HANNAH WARREN   Tammy Grimes
WILLIAM WARREN   George Grizzard

VISITOR from PHILADELPHIA
MARVIN MICHAELS   Jack Weston
BUNNY   Leslie Easterbrook
MILLIE MICHAELS   Barbara Barrie

VISITORS from LONDON
SIDNEY NICHOLS   George Grizzard
DIANA NICHOLS   Tammy Grimes

VISITORS from CHICAGO
MORT HOLLENDER   Jack Weston
BETH HOLLENDER   Barbara Barrie
STU FRANKLYN   George Grizzard
GERT FRANKLYN   Tammy Grimes

Directed by   Gene Saks
Scenery by   William Ritman
Lighting by   Tharon Musser
Costumes by   Jane Greenwood

CALIFORNIA SUITE is composed of four playlets whose action takes place in rooms 203 and 204 in the Beverly Hills Hotel.

Act One

SCENE ONE: *Visitor from New York*

Suite 203-4: a bedroom with an adjoining living room, and a bathroom off the bedroom. The décor is brightly colored and cheerful. Elegant reproductions of Van Gogh and Renoir hang on the walls. There are large color TV sets in both rooms, and a fireplace in the living room.

It is about one in the afternoon on a sunny, warm day in late fall. HANNAH WARREN *is standing at the window, arms folded, a cigarette in one hand, staring pensively out. She is in her early forties, an intelligent and sophisticated woman. She is wearing a tailored woolen suit, too warm for California, just right for New York—where she has just come from. Her packed suitcases are on the bed in the other room, ready for departure. The telephone rings.*

HANNAH (*Into the phone*) Yes? . . . Where are you? . . . Come on up. Room 203. (*She hangs up, takes another drag on her cigarette, then crushes it nervously into the ashtray. She picks up the phone again*) Room service, please. (*She waits tensely. Then, into the phone*) Hello? . . . This is Mrs. Warren in Suite 203 . . . I would like one tea with lemon and one double Scotch on the rocks . . . (*The phone in the bedroom rings*) Yes—203. Thank you. (*She hangs up. The other phone rings again. She goes into the bedroom, sits on the bed and answers the phone*) Yes? . . . Yes, it is . . . Hello? . . . Yes, Bob . . . Well, I was hoping to leave today. I have tickets on the three o'clock flight, but I don't think I'm going to make it . . . It can't be too soon for me . . . This entire city smells like an overripe cantaloupe . . . How is New York? . . . It is? . . . Snow—how wonderful! . . . No, no. The sun is shining, about eighty degrees, on Thanksgiving . . . truly disgusting. (*There is a knock on the living room door. She yells out*) Come in. It's open. (*Back into the phone, a little lower-voiced*) No, nothing's settled yet. But I'm not worried. (*The living room door opens.* WILLIAM WARREN *enters. He is about forty-five, quite attractive, well tanned and trim. He wears brush-denim slacks, an open sport shirt, a cashmere V-neck sweater and tan sneakers. He closes the door and inspects the room as she continues on the phone*) No, he just got here . . . I don't want to bring a lawyer into it yet. We'll see how this goes . . . When have you known me to be intimidated? (*She laughs*) Well, that doesn't count . . . Yes, I remember it in detail . . . You're wasting a perfectly good erotic conversation with my ex-husband in the other room and the operator probably listening . . . Yes, I will . . . As soon as he leaves . . . I do too . . . Bye. (*She hangs up and sits there a moment. She takes a pencil and jots down a note on the pad on the table next to the bed. She is not in any great hurry to greet her visitor. She gets up, gives herself another check in the mirror and goes to the doorway of the living room. He turns and they look at each other*) Sorry. I was on the phone. It's snowing in New York. We're going to have a white Thanksgiving. Don't you love it? (*She sits. He is still standing. He smiles*) Is that wonderful, warm smile for me?

BILLY   You still have trouble saying a simple "Hello."

HANNAH   Oh, I *am* sorry. You always did get a big thrill out of the "little" things in life . . . Hello, Bill.

BILLY (*With generous warmth*)   Hello, Hannah.

HANNAH   My God, look at you. You've turned into a young boy again.

BILLY   Have I?

HANNAH   Haven't you noticed? You look like the sweetest young fourteen-year-old boy. You're not spending your summers at camp, are you?

BILLY   Just three weeks in July. How are you?

HANNAH   Well, at this moment, nonplussed.

BILLY   Still the only one I know who can use "nonplussed" in regular conversation.

HANNAH   Don't be ridiculous, darling, I talk that way at breakfast . . . Turn around, let me look at you.

BILLY   Shouldn't we kiss or shake hands or something?

HANNAH   Let's save it for when you leave . . . I love your California clothes.

BILLY   They're Bloomingdale's, in New York.

HANNAH   The best place for California clothes. You look so . . . I don't know—what's the word I'm looking for?

BILLY   Happy?

HANNAH   Casual. It's so hard to tell out here—are you dressed up now, or is that sporty?

BILLY   I didn't think a tie was necessary for a reunion.

HANNAH   Is that what this is? When I walked in, I thought we were going to play tennis.

BILLY   Well, you look fit enough for it.

HANNAH   Fit? You think I look fit? What an awful shit you are. I look gorgeous.

BILLY   Yes, you do, Hannah. You look lovely.

HANNAH   No, no. *You* look lovely. *I* look gorgeous.

BILLY   Well, I lost about ten pounds.

HANNAH   Listen to what I'm telling you, you're *ravishing*. I love the way you're wearing your hair now. Where do you go, that boy who does Barbra Streisand?

BILLY   You like it, you can have my Thursday appointment with him . . . If you're interested, I'm feeling *very* well, thank you.

HANNAH   Well, of course you are. Look at that tan. Well, it's the life out here, isn't it? You have an office outdoors somewhere?

BILLY   No, just a desk near the window . . . Hey, Hannah, if we're going to banter like this, give me a little time. It's been nine years, I'm rusty.

HANNAH   You'll pick it right up again, it's like French. You see, that's what I would miss if I left New York. The bantering.

BILLY   San Francisco's only an hour away. We go up there and banter in emergencies.

HANNAH   Do you really?

BILLY   Would I lie to you?

HANNAH   I never liked San Francisco. I was always afraid I'd fall out of bed and roll down one of those hills.

BILLY   Not you, Hannah. You roll *up* hills.

HANNAH   Oh, good. You're bantering. The flight out wasn't a total loss . . . Aren't you going to sit down, Bill? Or do they call you Billy out here? Yes, they do. Jenny told me. Everybody calls you Billy.

BILLY (*Shrugs*) That's me. Billy.

HANNAH It's adorable. A forty-five-year-old Billy. Standing there in his cute little sneakers and sweater. Please, sit down, Billy, I'm beginning to feel like your math teacher.

BILLY I promised myself driving over here I would be pleasant. I am now being pleasant.

HANNAH You drive everywhere, do you?

BILLY Everywhere.

HANNAH Even to your car?

BILLY Would you mind if I called down for something to drink?

HANNAH It's done.

BILLY I don't drink double Scotches on the rocks any more. I gave up hard liquor.

HANNAH Oh? What would you like?

BILLY A cup of tea with lemon.

HANNAH It's done . . . No hard liquor? At all?

BILLY Not even wine. I'm big on apple juice.

HANNAH Cigarettes?

BILLY Gave them up.

HANNAH Don't you miss the coughing and the hacking in the morning?

BILLY I woke the dogs up. I have dogs now.

HANNAH Isn't divorce wonderful? . . . What about candy? Please don't tell me you've given up Snickers?

BILLY (*Shrugs*) Sorry.

HANNAH That *is* crushing news. You *have* changed, Billy. You've gone clean on me.

BILLY Mind *and* body. That doesn't offend you, does it?

HANNAH May they both live to be a thousand. I don't mean this to seem facetious, but how *do* you take care of yourself?

BILLY I watch my diet. I've cut out meat, and you *do* mean to be facetious. You're dying to make a little fun of me. I don't mind. I have an hour to kill . . . Would you believe I run five miles every morning?

HANNAH After what?

BILLY The newspaper. I have lazy dogs . . . Shall I keep going? I swim twenty laps every night when I come home from the studio. Eight sets of tennis every weekend. I sleep well. I haven't had a pill in three and a half years. I take vitamins and I eat natural, unprocessed health foods.

HANNAH Ah, aha! Health foods! At last, something in common.

BILLY Don't tell me you've given up P. J. Clarke's chili burgers?

HANNAH No, but I have them on whole wheat now . . . I'm enjoying this conversation. Tell me more about yourself. Jenny tells me you've taken up the banjo.

BILLY   The guitar. Classical *and* country.

HANNAH   Remarkable. And in New York you couldn't tune in Channel Five . . . More, more!

BILLY   I climb.

HANNAH   I beg your pardon?

BILLY   I climb. I climbed a ten-thousand-foot mountain in the Sierra Nevada last summer.

HANNAH   Well, that's no big deal. I climb that three times a week visiting my analyst.

BILLY   And no analyst.

HANNAH   Yes, I heard that. I'll accept the mountain climbing and, in a stretch, even the guitar. But no analyst? You ask too much, Billy. Why did you quit?

BILLY   I went sane.

HANNAH   Sane! How exciting. You mean you go out into the world every day all by yourself? (*He smiles, nods*) Don't you ever get depressed?

BILLY   Yes.

HANNAH   When?

BILLY   Now.

HANNAH   I'm so glad the sun hasn't dried up your brain completely . . . Tell me more news.

BILLY   I moved.

HANNAH   Oh, yes. You're not in Hardy Canyon any more.

BILLY Laurel. Laurel Canyon.

HANNAH Laurel, Hardy, what the hell? And where are you now?

BILLY Beverly Hills—a block north of Sunset Boulevard.

HANNAH What style house?

BILLY Very comfortable.

HANNAH Well, I'm sure it is. But what style is it?

BILLY Well, from the outside it looks like a small French farmhouse.

HANNAH A small French farmhouse. Just one block north of Sunset Boulevard. Sounds rugged . . . I passed something coming in from the airport. I thought it was a Moroccan villa—turned out to be a Texaco station.

BILLY We're a colorful community.

HANNAH I love it from the air.

BILLY And how is life over the subway?

HANNAH Fine. I still live in our old apartment. But you would hate it now.

BILLY What did you do to it?

HANNAH Not a thing.

BILLY And I heard you went in for an operation.

HANNAH A hysterectomy. I was out the same day. . . . And I believe you had prostate trouble.

BILLY Small world, isn't it?

HANNAH   Well, our past sins have a way of catching up with us . . . What else can I tell you about me?

BILLY   Jenny fills me in with everything.

HANNAH   Oh, I'm sure.

BILLY   I understand you have a new boyfriend.

HANNAH   A boyfriend? God forbid. I'm forty-two years old—I have a lover.

BILLY   Also a writer.

HANNAH   A newspaperman on the Washington *Post*.

BILLY   Really? Not one of those two who—

HANNAH   No.

BILLY   Right.

HANNAH   He's fifty-four. He has a heart condition, asthma and leans towards alcoholism. He also has the second-best mind I've met in this country since Adlai Stevenson . . . And what's with you, mate-wise?

BILLY   Mate-wise? Mate-wise I am seeing a very nice girl.

HANNAH   Are you? And where are you seeing her to?

BILLY   (*Annoyed*)   Oh, come on, Hannah.

HANNAH   What did I say? Have I offended you?

BILLY   Can we cut the cute chitchat? I think we've got other things to talk about?

HANNAH   I'm sorry. I *have* offended you.

BILLY   My God, it's been a long time since I've been involved in smart-ass conversation.

HANNAH   I beg *your* pardon, but *you* were the one who said things like "I hear you have a boyfriend" and "I'm seeing a very nice girl." I am *not* the one with the Bobbsey Twin haircut and the Peter Pan phraseology.

BILLY   I can see you've really come to hunt bear, haven't you?

HANNAH   Hunt bear? Did I actually hear you say "hunt bear"? Is that the kind of nifty conversation you have around those Sierra Nevada campfires?

BILLY   Forget the tea. Maybe I *will* have a double Scotch.

HANNAH   It's ordered. You're safe either way.

BILLY   Can we talk about Jenny?

HANNAH   What's your rush? She's only seventeen. She's got her whole life ahead of her. If I'm going to turn my daughter over to you—which I am not—at least I'd like to know what you're like.

BILLY   Jenny is *our* daughter! *Ours!*

HANNAH   Maybe. We'll see. They've been very slow with the blood test, (*They glare at each other a moment. She suddenly smiles*) So you live in a French farmhouse off Sunset Boulevard. Do you have a pool?

BILLY   Christ!

HANNAH   Come on, Billy, talk to me. I wrote down seventy-four questions to ask—don't make me look for the list. Do you have a pool? . . . Well, naturally you've got a pool. You've got a tan, so you've got a pool . . . Is it kidney shaped? . . . Liver? . . . Possibly gall bladder?

BILLY   Pancreas, actually. The head surgeon at Cedars of Lebanon put it in. You're terrific. You haven't spent fifteen days of your life out here, but you know exactly how we all live, don't you? Too bad you're going back so soon. You're gonna miss the way we spend our holidays. Wouldn't it *thrill* you to see a pink-painted Christmas tree on my lawn . . . or a three-flavored Baskin-Robbins snowman wearing alligator shoes . . . with a loudspeaker on the roof playing Sonny and Cher singing "Silent Night"?

HANNAH   When you've seen it once, the thrill is gone.

BILLY   Where's that drink?

HANNAH   What kind of a car do you have?

BILLY   You're really serious, aren't you?

HANNAH   I am *dead* serious. If I'm to leave my precious baby with you, I want to know what kind of a car I'm leaving her in.

BILLY   A brown Mercedes—450 SEL.

HANNAH   You have no class. You never had any class. A red *Pinto* in Beverly Hills would be class . . . Can I throw a few more questions at you?

BILLY   Questions? I thought they were spears.

HANNAH   What happened to your cute little wife? I don't mean *me*, I mean the cute one *after* me? Divorced her, too, didn't you?

BILLY   She was on the road a lot; I like to stay home. The first three years weren't too bad.

HANNAH   Oh, that's right, she was a singer, wasn't she? Somebody sent me one of her albums for Christmas, as a gag. They were right . . . I gagged.

BILLY   Really? She was number three on the charts, won two Grammys last year. I thought she was good.

HANNAH   Pity you didn't take up the guitar sooner, you could have still been with her . . . And tell me about the one you're seeing now. What does she do?

BILLY   She's an actress. Quite good. She was married before. Has a little boy, eleven years old.

HANNAH   And is marriage contemplated? . . . Am I being too nosy?

BILLY   Not for a *Newsweek* editor . . . Yes. Marriage is contemplated. It is being discussed; it is being considered. Strange as it seems, I like being married.

HANNAH   Right. And will there be room for all of you in the little French farmhouse, or will you have to move to an Italian *palazzo* on Wilshire Boulevard?

BILLY   What the hell are you so bitter about? You used to be bright and witty. Now you're just snide and sarcastic.

HANNAH   It comes with age. When you don't have a fast ball any more, you go to change-ups and sliders.

BILLY   Oh, please. Spare me your sports metaphors. You never knew a bunt from a double. The only reason you

went to the games is because you thought you looked
butch . . . Are you through with your interrogation?

HANNAH   I'm still interested in this new girl.

BILLY   Her name is Betsy LaSorda. Her father used to be
a damned good director. She can catch a trout and she
can beat me at tennis. I think she's peachy. What else?

HANNAH   Well, I know you've been bouncing around a
lot, Billy. Do you really care for her, or do you have
someone who gets you a break on marriage licenses?

BILLY   God, I can just hear the quips flying when you and
the second-best mind since Adlai Stevenson get together.
Sitting there freezing under a blanket at the Washington
Redskin game playing anagrams with the names of all
the Polish players . . . I'll tell you something, Hannah:
For one of the brightest women in America, you bore
the hell out of me. Your mind clicks off bric-a-bracs so
goddamn fast, it never has a chance to let an honest emo-
tion or thought ever get through.

HANNAH   And you're so *filled* with honest emotions, you
fall in love every time someone sings a ballad. You're
worse than a hopeless romantic, you're a *hopeful* one.
You're the kind of a man who would end the world's
famine problem by having them all eat out . . . prefera-
bly at a good Chinese restaurant!

BILLY   (*Gets up, starts towards the door, stops*)   What
do you want to do about Jenny?

HANNAH   Who?

BILLY   Do you want to discuss this problem sensibly and sincerely, or do you want to challenge me to the *New York Times* crossword puzzle for her?

HANNAH   Oh, stop pouting. You may dress like a child, but you don't have to act like one.

BILLY   Would you mind terribly if I said "Up yours" and left?

HANNAH   What have you done to her, Billy? She's changed. She used to come back to New York after the summers here taller and anxious to see her friends . . . Now she meditates and eats alfalfa.

BILLY   She just turned seventeen. Something was bound to happen to her.

HANNAH   You have no legal rights to her, of course. You understand that.

BILLY   Certainly.

HANNAH   Then tell her to come home with me.

BILLY   I did. She would like to try it with me for a year. She's not happy in New York, Hannah.

HANNAH   *Nobody's* happy in New York. But they're *alive.*

BILLY   I can't fight you. If you want to take her, then take her. But I think you'd be making a mistake.

HANNAH   She still has another year of high school left.

BILLY   Believe it or not, they have good schools here. I can show you some, if you like.

HANNAH   Oh, that should be fun. Something like the Universal Studio tour?

BILLY   What a snob you are.

HANNAH   Thank God there's a few of us left.

BILLY   What is there so beautiful about your life that makes it so important to put down everyone else's? Forty square blocks bounded by Lincoln Center on the west and Cinema II on the east is not the center of the goddamn universe. I grant you it's an exciting, vibrant, stimulating, fabulous city, but it is not Mecca . . . It just smells like it.

HANNAH   The hell with New York! Or Boston or Washington or Philadelphia. I don't care *where* Jenny lives, but *how*. She's an intelligent girl with a good mind. Let it grow and prosper. But what the hell is she going to learn in a community that has valet parking just to pick up four bagels and the *Hollywood Reporter?*

BILLY   I've been to Martha's Vineyard in July, Hannah. Heaven protect me from another intellectual Cape Cod summer . . . The political élite queueing up in old beach sandals to see Bogart pictures, standing there eating ice cream cones and reading the *New Republic*.

HANNAH   Neat, wasn't it?

BILLY   No. Your political friends never impressed me . . . I remember one hot Sunday afternoon in Hyannisport when our ambassador to some war-torn Middle Eastern country was in a state of despair because he couldn't get the hang of throwing a Frisbee. My God, the absurdity

. . . I went to a charity luncheon in East Hampton to raise money for the California grape pickers. There was this teeming mob of women who must have spent a total of twelve thousand dollars on new Gucci pants in order to raise two thousand dollars for the grape pickers . . . Why the hell didn't they just mail them the pants?

HANNAH You were terrific when you used to write like that. . . . I didn't see the last picture you wrote, but they tell me it grossed very well in backward areas.

BILLY Jesus, was I anything like you before?

HANNAH I couldn't hold a candle to you.

BILLY No wonder no one spoke to me here for the first two years.

HANNAH Lucky you.

BILLY Look, I don't want to interrupt your train of venom, but could we get back to Jenny?

HANNAH Jenny. Yes, what a good idea.

BILLY If you respect her as a person, respect her right to make a free choice.

HANNAH You get her for the summers, that's enough. If the judge had seen your life-style, you'd be lucky to get her Labor Day afternoon.

BILLY Funny how we haven't discussed *your* life-style, isn't it?

HANNAH I don't have a life-style. I have a life.

BILLY   The hell you do. The only time you're alive is Tuesday mornings when the magazine hits the stands . . . You're a voyeur in newsprint, snooping on everyone else's life-style and editing out the healthy aspects of the human condition because, for a dollar a copy, who the hell wants to read about happiness?

HANNAH   Sometimes I actually miss you. You wouldn't consider coming back East and entering into a ménage à trois?

BILLY   Would you like to know what Jenny has to say about you?

HANNAH   She's told me. She thinks I'm a son-of-a-bitch. She also thinks I'm a *funny* son-of-a-bitch. She loves me but she doesn't like me. She's afraid of me. She's intimidated by me. She respects me but wouldn't want to become like me. We have a normal mother and daughter relationship.

BILLY   She told me she feels stifled—that the only time she can really breathe freely is when she's out here.

HANNAH   I have a wonderful nose and throat man on East Eighty-fourth Street.

BILLY   How the hell can you be so flippant when it comes to your own daughter's well-being?

HANNAH   And how the hell can you be so *pompous* not to recognize a very healthy rebellious attitude in an adolescent? If she *didn't* complain, I would probably send her to an expensive shrink. Since she's with *me* ten month's of the year, it's only natural *you're* the one she's going to miss . . . I think by and large she and I have managed quite well but it's obvious, like all young girls, she needs a father image. I don't mind. If it's only July and August, it might as well be you.

BILLY This is Thanksgiving and she came out *without* your permission.

HANNAH She never had a very good head for dates.

BILLY What would you do if I just kept her here with me?

HANNAH Don't be ridiculous.

BILLY But what would you do, Hannah?

HANNAH I would find the very best lawyer I could in California . . . and have him beat the shit out of you.

BILLY Would you drag it through the courts if I said I'm keeping her for six months?

HANNAH I will call my friend, the Attorney General of the United States, if she is not on that three o'clock plane.

BILLY (*Sits back and smiles at her*) Why didn't you ever run for office, Hannah? I always thought you'd make a helluva Governor.

HANNAH Because I don't think a democratic system really works. Offer me a monarchy and we'll talk. (*Looks at her watch*) It's one fifteen. Will you call Jenny or shall I?

BILLY No.

HANNAH No what?

BILLY No, *sir!*

HANNAH If you'll tell me how to get to your little French farmhouse, I'll pick her up myself.

BILLY How much time do you spend with her? Do you ever have breakfast with her? How many nights does she eat dinner alone? Do you think she's really happy with that twenty-dollar bill you give her every time you go off to Washington for the weekend? The girl is growing up lonely, Hannah, and if you tell me she's got a cat and a canary, I'll belt you right in the choppers.

HANNAH She has two dogs, a Dominican cook and twelve different girls who sleep over every time I'm away. Despite her Gothic reports, she is not living the life of Jane Eyre.

BILLY The truth, Hannah . . . You know if we leave it up to Jenny, you don't stand a chance in hell of getting her on that plane. Right?

HANNAH Certainly. Why else would the ninny run away? . . . Who said we don't have problems? She is seventeen years old, and when we go at each other, she needs another shoulder to cry on . . . But I'll be goddamned if I'm giving up a daughter for a cashmere shoulder three thousand miles away.

BILLY My God, you're really afraid . . . This is an event. I think it's the first time I've ever actually seen you nervous.

HANNAH Wrong. I was nervous on our wedding night . . . Unfortunately, it was *after* we had sex.

BILLY Please. No cheap shots. It's not like you. I mean, we may have had a very narrow chance for happiness, but sex was never a stumbling block.

HANNAH Neither was it an architectural marvel . . . Oh, I'm not blaming *you*. Actually you were very skillful in bed. You could ravage me for hours without ever mussing the sheets. But the moment it was over, you would heave a deep sigh and tell me your plans for the future . . . The sex was stimulating but the plans were so freaking boring.

BILLY Boring? And I have made love to women with the television on before, but *never* watching Eric Sevareid.

HANNAH Sometimes we need our private fantasies to help us get to the top of Magic Mountain.

BILLY You know something, Hannah? . . . I don't like you any more.

HANNAH It's okay. I'm not always fond of me either . . . What are we going to do, Billy? I want my daughter back. You're the only one who can help me.

BILLY (*Looks at her*) You're being sincere now, aren't you? . . . What a shame. You do it so seldom, when it finally comes I'm *still* waiting for the zingers.

HANNAH Billy . . . what do you look forward to?

BILLY (*He looks behind him*) Where did *that* non sequitur come from?

HANNAH You know me. My mind is always on "express." I'd really like to know. You're forty-five years old, you've been married twice, had a child, a half a dozen houses, a promising journalistic career and some questionable but undeniably commercial successes . . . I'd like to know what it is you look forward to.

BILLY (*Pauses*)   Saturdays . . . I love Saturdays.

HANNAH   For a simple-minded bastard, sometimes you sure are smart . . . You know what I look forward to?

BILLY   What?

HANNAH   Christ, it's hard for me to say it . . . Are you going to laugh?

BILLY   Only if it's not funny. What do you look forward to?

HANNAH   I look forward to a granddaughter . . . I think I screwed up the first time.

BILLY (*Good-naturedly*)   No one can phrase sentiment like you.

HANNAH   Are you going to help me?

BILLY   By sending Jenny home? She'd be back in two weeks.

HANNAH   Not if I put heavy weights on her feet . . . Offer me a suggestion, goddamn it, for old times' sake.

BILLY   You know my suggestion.

HANNAH   I only have one more year with her. In September she'll go to college. In four years she'll come out a revolutionary or a nun . . . or even worse, like you or me.

BILLY A little bit of both wouldn't be so bad.

HANNAH Do you like your mother?

BILLY She's dead.

HANNAH Don't quibble. Did you like her?

BILLY For a neurotic woman, she wasn't too bad.

HANNAH I don't like mine much. Can you imagine being a pain in the ass for seventy-eight years? I felt something was wrong even when I was in the womb. I never felt comfortable. I think I was hanging too low . . . We shouldn't have had Jenny. People like you and me are too selfish . . . I don't want her to grow up hating me and I don't want her growing up here, because I'm liable to hate her . . . Maybe you and I should have stayed together and we could have let *Jenny* go. What do you think?

BILLY I changed my mind. I think I like you again.

HANNAH He's not going to live very long, you know.

BILLY Who isn't?

HANNAH My Washington *Post* friend. He had open heart surgery that was a total waste of time.

BILLY I'm sorry to hear that.

HANNAH Me, too . . . The man could really make me laugh.

BILLY Sounded like it was pretty good.

HANNAH Oh, well, you win some, you lose some.

BILLY (*With admiration*) Talk about resiliency . . .

HANNAH For a smart lady in a man's world, I'm not doing too bad.

BILLY No, you're not . . . Would it comfort you any to meet my actress friend? Just to know that Jenny hasn't fallen into wicked hands?

HANNAH I'm shaky enough right now—I don't have to meet someone with smoother skin than me . . . Thanks a lot.

BILLY For what?

HANNAH You're supposed to say, "She doesn't have smoother skin than you."

BILLY Sorry, she does. It's only in good conversation she comes in second place.

HANNAH The truth . . . Is being in love better now?

BILLY Yes.

HANNAH Why?

BILLY Because it's now.

HANNAH I don't like the way this meeting is going. I think I'm losing ground. Why don't we go to New York and finish it?

BILLY You can have it both ways, you know.

HANNAH What does that mean?

BILLY Take your summer vacation this winter. Come out here, I'll find you a nice place at the beach. This way we can both see Jenny.

HANNAH   Two months? Out *here?* . . . I would get con-
stipation of the mind.

BILLY   You're afraid.

HANNAH   Of what?

BILLY   That you might like it. You're afraid you might
like *anything.* Happiness is so banal, isn't it?

HANNAH   No. Just that statement . . . Let's keep things
the way they are, Billy. God only meant us to have nine
years together. He knew what He was doing.

BILLY   Well, then we haven't settled anything, have we?

HANNAH   Well, we've settled that I'm not coming out
here for two months. It was worth coming out here just
to settle that. That only leaves Jenny to deal with.

BILLY   Shall I get her up here? She's downstairs in the car
with her bags packed . . . She's willing to abide by any
decision we both make.

HANNAH   Oh, what a cunning bastard you are. If we say
she goes back to New York, she'll think I coerced you.
And if we say stay here, she'll think I didn't even put up
a fight for her.

BILLY   Do you think she has that devious a mind?

HANNAH   Certainly. *She's my* daughter . . . I don't suppose *you'd* consider spending two months back East?

BILLY   Only if everyone there leaves . . . You want me to
make it easy for you, Hannah? I'll throw in my vote.
Whatever you say goes. And I'll tell Jenny we *both*
made the decision.

HANNAH (*Really perplexed*)   Jesus, no wonder there are so many used car salesmen out here. How much time do I have? I was never very good with deadlines.

BILLY   As much time as you want.

HANNAH (*Goes over to the window and looks out, trying to see if she can see his car*)   Which is your car? They're *all* Mercedes. (*She turns; he is staring at her*) What are you looking at me like that for?

BILLY   It's not often I've seen you looking so vulnerable.

HANNAH   Well, take a picture of it. You won't see it again . . . Keep her.

BILLY   What?

HANNAH   I said, keep her—six months, not a year. And *I* pick the school. And whoever I pick, they have to send me three references . . . Christ, what am I doing?

BILLY   Stay the weekend, Hannah. Talk it over with Jenny. You don't have to decide because you've got a plane ticket.

HANNAH   I'm a fighter, Billy. If I stay the weekend, I not only take Jenny with me, but I'll take your new girl-friend back, too.

BILLY   Hannah, don't let me bully you into this. Why can't the three of us talk it over? Let me get Jenny up here.

HANNAH   *No*, goddamn it! If I have to give her up to get her back, then let's do it.

BILLY   You mean it? You'll let her stay?

HANNAH   You think you're in for a picnic? Wait'll you try shopping for clothes with her.

BILLY   Can you take a compliment? You're not the Hannah I left nine years ago.

HANNAH   And I'm missing the ovaries to prove it . . .

BILLY   Well, guess who's nonplussed now?

HANNAH   Jesus, you never thought I would say yes, did you? You know, I don't think you're prepared to take on your own daughter. Watching her swim for eight weeks at the beach is not the same as being a parent . . . Don't look now, Billy, but you just lost your sun tan.

BILLY   If you think I'm scared, you're damned right.

HANNAH   I love it. Oh, God I love it. Wait'll you see how she eats in the winter. You'll be dead broke by Christmas.

BILLY   I think you're doing a terrific thing, Hannah.

HANNAH   So do I.

BILLY   And if for any reason, I feel things aren't working out, I'll send her back to you.

HANNAH   The hell you will. You're a Father now, Billy.

BILLY   I suppose you want to see her before you leave.

HANNAH   Well, you suppose wrong. I've seen her. I'll call her when I get to New York.

BILLY   What should I tell her?

HANNAH   Tell her I hope she'll be very happy and that I'm selling her record collection.

BILLY   (*He starts towards the door*) You know, we couldn't have been too bad together. We produced a hell of a girl.

HANNAH   You got that a little wrong . . . I think the two of you produced a hell of a mother.

BILLY   Maybe you're right . . . Can we shake hands now? I'm about to leave.

HANNAH   Sure. Why not? What more can I lose? (*They shake hands. He holds on to hers*) Serve her plenty of broccoli and lima beans.

BILLY   She likes them?

HANNAH   *Hates* them. But from now on, what do I care?

BILLY   Goodbye, Hannah . . . It was good seeing you again.

HANNAH   (*On the point of tears*)   I suddenly feel like an artist selling a painting he doesn't want to part with.

BILLY   (*Gently*)   I'll frame it and keep it in a good light.

HANNAH   Do that . . . And take care of Jenny, too. (BILLY *looks at her, puts his hands on her shoulders, and kisses her on the cheek. He wants to say something else, then changes his mind, opens the door quickly and leaves. She stands there a moment, then moves back to the window and looks down. Then she goes to the phone and picks up the receiver. Into the phone. About to break down)* Operator . . . Get me room service . . . I never got my goddamn drinks.

(*The lights dim*)

Blackout

SCENE TWO: *Visitor from Philadelphia*

The morning sunlight is streaming in through the opened drapes in the living room. By contrast, the bedroom is very dark, barely visible. The curtains and shades are drawn. We hear a long, loud, male yawn from the bed.

MARVIN Oh, God . . . (*He rubs his face with both hands*) Ohhhhhhhhhh. (*He gets up and goes into the bathroom, moving almost zombie-like as he feels the awfulness of his hangover.* MARVIN MICHAELS *is about forty-two. He wears undershorts, T-shirt and one black sock. His hair is rumpled. We hear him gargle. He comes out of the bathroom, goes back to the bed, gets in and sits up*) Ugh, never again . . . Never never never . . . (*He sits there trying to breathe, and suddenly, from under the sheets, an arm comes. A female arm. He recoils, frightened to death*) Oh, God . . . (*He lifts the hand to his face and looks at it. He lifts the cover back, and we see a woman, who, from what we can make out, seems to be attractive. She is wearing the tops of his pajamas*) What are you doing here? I thought you left! (*There is no response from her: she is out like a light*) Hey! (*He nudges her*) Hey, come on, you can't stay here! Hey, wake up! (*He turns, gropes for his watch on the night table, and looks at it*) Eleven o'clock! Jesus Christ, it's eleven o'clock! (*He jumps out of bed*) Wake up! Come on, get up, it's eleven o'clock, don't you understand? (*He turns back and reaches for the phone*) Crazy! I must be crazy! (*Into the phone*) Operator? . . . What time is it? . . . (*Screams*) Eleven o'clock? . . . Why didn't you call me? . . . I left a wake-up call for eight o'clock . . . I *did!* . . . Mr. Michaels, Room 203, an eight o'clock wake-up call . . . I *didn't?* . . . I can't understand that . . . Never mind, did I get any calls? . . . Well, take the hold signal off, I'm taking calls. (*He hangs up*) How could I forget to leave a wake-up call? (*He nudges the girl, then starts getting dressed*) Hey, come on. Get up, will ya? You have to get dressed. My wife could walk in any minute. Eleven o'clock—her plane probably got in already. (*He gets his pants and other sock on*) *Will you get up? We got an emergency here!* (*He puts his shirt on. The girl hasn't moved*) What's wrong with you? You deaf or something? (*He crosses to the bed. She is breathing but not moving*) Are you all right? (*He nudges her again. She moans but doesn't move. He turns and looks at the floor next to the bed, and picks up a quart-size empty bottle of vodka*) Oh, God, what did you do? An entire bottle of vodka? You drank a whole bottle of vodka with my wife coming in? Are you crazy? (*He nudges her*) Are you all right? Can you hear me? (*She moans*) What? What did you say? . . . I couldn't hear that. (*She moans again. He puts his ear to her mouth*) Sick . . . You feel sick? . . . Six margaritas and a bottle of vodka, I wonder why . . . Listen, you can get dressed and take a cab home and be nice and sick in your own bed all day . . . Doesn't that sound nice? Heh? (*No response*) Oh, God, what am I going to do? . . . Water. You want a little water? (*He rushes to the table, pours a glass of ice water and rushes back to her*) Here, lady. Sip a little cold water. (*He picks her head up and tries to pour some water into her mouth, but her lips won't open and it dribbles down her face)* Drink, sweetheart . . . for my sake . . . Open your lips, you crazy broad! (*To himself*) Don't panic . . . Panic is the quickest way to divorce—mustn't panic! (*He sticks his fingers in the glass and flicks water at her face*) Up, up, up! Here we go! Rise and shine, everybody up! (*He throws more water. She doesn't budge. He shakes her shoulders—she flops about like a ragdoll*) Move! Please God, make her move. I'll never be a bad person again as long as I live. (*She doesn't move; she lies there*) All right, we're gonna get you dressed and down into a cab. Once you're on your feet, you'll be fine . . . I'm really sorry this happened. I don't remember much, but it must have been a wonderful evening, whatever your name is . . . Could you help me a little, honey? Please? . . . You're not gonna help me. All right, Marvin, think. Think, Marvin. (*He slaps his own face to help him think*) I gotta get outta here. (*He picks up phone*) Operator, get me the front desk. (*He looks at the girl,* BUNNY) I have two wonderful children who need a father—don't do this to me. (*Into the phone*) Hello? . . . This is an *angry* Mr. Michaels in Suite 203 and 4 . . . Listen, I am very uncomfortable in my room . . . The toilet kept dripping all night. No, I don't want it fixed. I want another room. I could move out immediately . . . I'm expecting my wife in from Philadelphia any minute, and I *know* she's not going to be happy once she sees this room . . . *Who*'s here? . . . MY WIFE? MY-WIFE-IS-HERE? . . . You sent my wife up without calling me? . . . How could you do such a thing? What the hell kind of a cheap hotel are you running here? . . . Can't you send someone to stop her? She's not going to like this room! (*There is a knock on the living room door. He slams the phone down and dashes around the bedroom in a frenzy*) Oh, God! (*Whispers to the inert form*) Oh, God! Oh, God! OH, GOD! OH, GOD! OH, GOD! Listen to me . . . I have to go into the other room. When I'm inside, lock the door from in here. Don't open it for anyone, do you understand? . . . For anyone! (*Another knock on the door. He goes into the living room, closing the bedroom door. Then asks softly and innocently*) Who is it?

MILLIE It's me.

MARVIN Millie?

MILLIE Yes.
(*He picks up a full ashtray and two champagne glasses and hurls them out the sliding door to the patio. He opens the door*)

MARVIN Hello, sweetie.

MILLIE Hello. What took you so long? Why didn't you pick me up at the airport?

MARVIN Why?

MILLIE Yes, why?

MARVIN Why . . . I've been sick all night. I threw up in the other room. Don't go in there. The doctor just left ten minutes ago. I have acute gastroenteritis . . . It's nothing to worry about.

MILLIE Oh, my God. When did this happen?

MARVIN   About two o'clock in the morning.

MILLIE   What did you eat?

MARVIN   Spaghetti with white clam sauce—and tacos . . .
It was a Mexican-Italian restaurant.

MILLIE   Spaghetti with tacos?

MARVIN   And some tortillas parmegan. Two people got
sick at the next table. I thought it was the flu. I never
had that kind of food before.

MILLIE   Where did you get a doctor?

MARVIN   I called my brother. He got me a wonderful
stomach man. Greasiest restaurant I ever saw . . . Even
the napkins kept slipping off the table.

MILLIE   You look terrible. Why don't you get into bed?
You'll feel more comfortable.

MARVIN   I'm not supposed to lie down. It makes me nau-
seous . . . I feel a lot better in this room. It's cheerier
. . . I need some Compazine spansules.

MILLIE   What's that?

MARVIN   It stops nausea. Compazine spansules.

MILLIE   Did you call the drugstore?

MARVIN   They don't carry it. It has codeine in it. The
nearest place that has it is a drugstore on Santa Monica
Boulevard. But they don't deliver. I'll have to go over
there myself. I'm just nervous about throwing up in the
taxi.

MILLIE   All right, I'll go. Where's the prescription?

MARVIN   What prescription?

MILLIE   Didn't the doctor give you a prescription? They're not gonna give you codeine without a prescription.

MARVIN   Yes, they will. In California they will . . . Compazine spansules.
   (*He grabs his stomach*)

MILLIE   If you don't need a prescription, just send the cab driver. I'm exhausted. I just flew in from Philadelphia.

MARVIN   They tell me you can't trust the cab drivers out here. They're notorious for going for medicine and not coming back . . . Oh, God, what I'd give for a good Compazine spansule.

MILLIE   What are you going to do about the bar mitzvah?

MARVIN   Oh, we're going. I didn't fly all the way from Philadelphia to miss my nephew's bar mitzvah . . . I'm glad you reminded me. Harry called a few minutes ago. He wants us to get over to the temple as soon as possible, so why don't you go down for a cab and I'll finish getting dressed.

MILLIE   It's just after eleven. I thought we didn't have to be there until one.

MARVIN   That's for the others. Harry wants us to get a seat down front. His kid has a very soft voice and he doesn't want us to miss his speech. So why don't you go down and get the cab and I'll finish getting dressed.

MILLIE   And what am I going to wear?

MARVIN   What do you mean? Didn't you bring a dress? I told you to bring a dress.

MILLIE   They lost it. (*Starts to cry*) They can't find my luggage.

MARVIN   Who can't?

MILLIE   The airlines. They lost my luggage. My new suitcase with my new dress and my new shoes. I have nothing to wear.
   (*She sobs*)

MARVIN   (*Exaggerated anger*)   Lost your luggage? Your good luggage that I gave you for Christmas? My God, that gets me insane! In this day and age, to still lose luggage . . .

MILLIE   They said they'll call me at the hotel when they find it. I just wanted to come back here, take a hot bath and a nap.

MARVIN   There's no time for a nap. I know those airlines. You've got to go down there and make a fuss. Call a cab. We're going back to the airport *right now* and demand satisfaction.

MILLIE   I don't want satisfaction. I want my bar mitzvah dress.

MARVIN   We'll go shopping in Beverly Hills. This is the best time of day, before they get crowded.

MILLIE   This trip is costing us a fortune. Why did you take a suite? It's so expensive.

MARVIN I wanted you to be comfortable. To celebrate—our first trip to California . . . It was a mistake. The bedroom is stifling. It's all those vines outside the window—you can't breathe. I'm going to tell them to close off the bedroom and we'll just keep this room. *This* is cheerful.

MILLIE (*Looks around*) There are no beds in this room.

MARVIN Oh, I didn't know you wanted to stay over. I thought we were going up to San Francisco right after the bar mitzvah.

MILLIE The same day? Then when will I see Los Angeles?

MARVIN There's not much to see. I mean, there aren't that many points of interest.

MILLIE The third largest city in the United States?

MARVIN Only in population. There's plenty of *people* to see, but we don't know any of them.

MILLIE Three thousand miles just to see a bar mitzvah? I've seen them before—they're not worth that much of a trip. Don't you ever do this to me again.

MARVIN (*Guiltily*) Do what? What? Don't do what again?

MILLIE Make us take separate planes—for what? We're so worried that something is going to happen to us and our children will be left alone. So look what happens to us separately. They lose my luggage and you have gastroenteritis. (*She gets up*) I have to go to the bathroom.

MARVIN (*Screeches*)   NOW? (*He races around to block the door to the bedroom and bathroom*)

MILLIE   I haven't gone in four hours; *now* is a good time.

MARVIN   I just told you. I threw up in there. I mean, everywhere—the bathtub, the floor, the mirror. I wouldn't let you go in there.

MILLIE   I've seen you get sick before.

MARVIN   Not on a holiday. Not on a vacation. I think on a holiday one should try to preserve *some* sense of romanticism . . . At *home*, I wouldn't mind.

MILLIE   I can't *wait* till we get home. You're acting very peculiar. Are you sure you don't have a fever or something?

MARVIN   It's possible . . . The doctor said I might be getting periods of fever and periods of not knowing how certain inexplicable events may have happened.

MILLIE   What inexplicable events?

MARVIN (*Shrugs*)   I don't know . . . I mean, in case some trivial thing comes up that I can't explain. The doctor said that's very possible.

MILLIE   I don't understand a word you're saying.

MARVIN   Exactly my point.

MILLIE   I have to go to the bathroom.

MARVIN   *Please* . . . Give me the opportunity of making it presentable first. It means a lot to me.

MILLIE   We've been married fifteen years, and you've never cleaned up a bathroom for me before.

MARVIN   Well, I think it's high time I started. (*He kisses her cheek*) I'll be right out . . . Why don't you thumb through the brochure and find us a nice restaurant for tomorrow? Anything but Mexican-Italian. (MILLIE *goes over to the desk and thumbs through the brochure. He goes into the bedroom, locks the door behind him, and rushes to the bed. The girl is still out like a light. He starts to pick her up*) I'm sorry. I don't like doing this, but I'm going to have to leave you out in the hall. (*He drags her towards the door*) You'll be all right, they'll take care of you. They have *wonderful* service here. (*He gets to the door and opens it with one hand, propping her up behind his back. He sticks his head out, sees somebody*) OH! Jesus, you scared me. Hello, how are you?

> (*He keeps nodding, then pulls the girl away so as not to be seen and closes the door. He starts back for the bed and dumps her on it. Meanwhile in the living room,* MILLIE *is pacing around in her discomfort at needing to use the john. Finally she knocks on the bedroom door*)

MILLIE   Marvin? . . . Marvin, the door is locked.

MARVIN   I CAN'T HEAR YOU! I'M IN THE BATH-ROOM.

> (*He drags the "body" back to the bed and starts to cover it with blankets. He wrestles with her legs to get them to lie flat, and frantically smoothes the bed-covers*)

MILLIE   Open the door. Why is this door locked?

MARVIN   It's not locked. Maybe it's stuck.
(*Once the girl is completely covered, he hides her shoes and other female articles under the bed*)

MILLIE   Well, *open it*, for God's sakes.

MARVIN   I'm not through in the bathroom yet.

MILLIE   I want to come in the *bed*room! Will you open this door?

MARVIN   OPEN THE WHAT?

MILLIE   The door, the door.
(*This kind of exchange continues until* MARVIN *is ready to open the door*)

MARVIN   You see? It was open. Don't you know how to work a door?

MILLIE   What took you so long? What's the matter, you got a girl in here?

MARVIN   (*Playing along with her joke*) That's right. I got a cute redhead in the bed! . . . I cleaned up the bathroom. You can go in there now.

MILLIE   It's a nice bedroom. I wish we didn't have to move.

MARVIN   I know. Isn't that a shame? (*She closes the bathroom door behind her.* MARVIN *rushes around the room trying to think of how he can dispose of the girl. He looks at the closet, opens it and gets in to see if the body will fit, then he rushes to the bed, hurls the covers off*

*and picks up the helpless girl. He gets her halfway out
of the bed when he hears the john flush)* I'll never make
it.

(*He puts the body back into the bed, covers her with
sheets and blankets, presses down and flattens her,
then arranges himself elaborately on the edge of the
bed to conceal the girl, as the bathroom door opens
and* MILLIE *comes out*)

MILLIE   I love the telephone in the john.

MARVIN   It's fun, isn't it? Would you like to go back in
there and call the kids?

MILLIE   Why? I just left the kids and I just used the john
. . . How you feeling?

MARVIN   Not as good as I would like . . . I was thinking,
maybe you could take a shower and I could take a nap
for about an hour. We have plenty of time. And maybe
by then they'll find your luggage.

MILLIE   My God, I hope so. Let's *both* take a nap.

MARVIN   (*Stunned*)   You mean together?

MILLIE   Don't we always?

MARVIN   No, no. We *sleep* together. Naps I usually take
alone.

MILLIE   (*Starts toward the bed*)   I never heard you talk
so crazy . . . Move over. I'm going to lie down.

MARVIN   (*Sits up quickly*)   NO! No, please. I—I want
you to sit down a minute. I have something to tell you,
Millie.

MILLIE   You can't tell me lying down?

MARVIN   It's the kind of thing you should hear sitting up.

MILLIE (*Shrugs*)   You want me to sit up, I'll sit up.
   (*She sits in the armchair, takes off her shoes*)

MARVIN   Millie, you mean more to me than you could possibly know . . . but sometimes we transgress. Sometimes we do foolish little things that unwittingly may cause hurt and injury to the other.

MILLIE   I don't think you've ever consciously hurt me.

MARVIN   Consciously, no. But a careless word here, a thoughtless gesture there . . .

MILLIE   Nothing major, Marvin. We've had our disagreements, but nothing major.

MARVIN   I'm glad you brought that up, Millie . . . What would you consider major?

MILLIE   Major? . . . I don't know . . . I couldn't picture you doing anything "major." A couple of minors maybe, but no major.

MARVIN   But if I did . . . If I were not my normal self— temporarily—if illness had caused me to act in some foolish manner, what hurt could I cause you that was major?

MILLIE   It's so hard to say . . . I guess if you were cruel to the children, I think that would be major.

MARVIN (*Jumping on it*)   I would put that Number One! I think that would be the worst thing a man could do to

his wife in a marriage. To be cruel to their children is unpardonable . . . *All else* could be forgiven.
(*He looks at the bed*)

MILLIE   And if I caught you with another woman. That would be major.

MARVIN   Let's not get off the children thing so fast! Children are the reflection of the love that two people share . . . Children are the emanations of the spirit of love that—

MILLIE   My back is killing me from the plane. I've got to lie down for a few minutes.
(*She gets up, going towards the bed*)

MARVIN (*He jumps up in front of her*)   Let's make love in the living room.

MILLIE   What?

MARVIN   Let's make love on the living room sofa—like we did on our honeymoon in Florida.

MILLIE   That was a love seat.
(*She starts for the bedroom*)

MARVIN (*Trying to distract her*)   How about on the rug? The living room rug. I could order up some champagne. It's been so long since we made love on a rug.

MILLIE   That's not a rug. It's carpeting. I don't like to make love on carpeting.

MARVIN   Oh, come on. (*He lies flat on the floor*) It's a holiday. We're going to be middle-aged soon.

MILLIE   What's the matter with the bed? We've always done very well with a bed.

MARVIN   I'm just trying to think of something *different* . . . to break up the monotony of a bed.
   (*She crosses into the bedroom*)

MILLIE (*Hurt*)   I didn't think our love-making was so monotonous.
   (*He follows her*)

MARVIN   It *isn't!* Our love-making is *wonderful!* It's the bed that get repetitious. (*Holds his stomach*) I think I'm getting another attack.

MILLIE (*Angry*)   Well, who tells you to eat Mexican-Italian food? You're not the only one who's feeling sick . . . I'm sick, too. (*Starts to cry*) I got my period on the plane . . . The first vacation we've had together in two years and I have to get my goddamn period, so don't tell me how sick you are!
   (*She suddenly sobs and falls onto the bed, crying into the pillow. She lies right next to the hidden body underneath. He watches in terror*)

MARVIN (*Screams*)   NO!

MILLIE (*She sits up, then gets off bed and looks at him queerly*)   Well, you don't have to be *that* upset. It's not my fault. I didn't time out your lousy nephew's bar mitzvah . . . I'm sorry! I'm sorry, Marvin. I didn't mean to say that. I'm just so cranky and irritable. You know I always get that way when I get my period.

MARVIN   I know.

MILLIE (*She sits back on the bed and lies down*)　Come here, Marvin. Just lie down with me and hold me. We don't have to make love. Just hold me and tell me you're not upset that I'm so irritable. (*He lies down on the floor near the bed*).

MILLIE (*Looks down at him*)　Marvin, why don't you get into the bed?

MARVIN (*He gets up, walks away*)　Millie, I can't keep this up any more. I'm going to get a heart attack . . . I've got to tell you something.

MILLIE　What, Marvin? What is it, darling?

MARVIN　It was never my intention to hurt you, Millie, but it's very possible in the next few minutes you may be terribly, terribly hurt.

MILLIE　Is it major or minor?

MARVIN　To me it was minor, to you I think it's going to be extremely major.

MILLIE　Tell me, Marvin . . . It couldn't be that bad, as long as you're not trying to cover up something.
　　(BUNNY *unconsciously pushes the covers down and reveals herself—but at that moment* MILLIE *is facing the other way*)

MARVIN (*Alarmed, he looks up at the ceiling because he doesn't know where else to look;* MILLIE *looks up also*)　There's something I'd like to show you, Millie. But I'm going to ask you to do something for me first . . . Say nothing for ten seconds. Whatever comes to mind, please, for the sake of both of us, say nothing for ten seconds . . . You may turn around now, Millie.

(*She turns her head around to the right and sees the body in the bed. She looks at it, and suddenly laughs aloud*)

MILLIE   One . . . two . . . three . . . I'm praying, Marvin . . . I'm praying the maid came in here to clean, got dizzy from overwork and fainted in your bed . . . I pray to God the maids in this hotel wear pajamas.

MARVIN   It's not the maid, Millie.

MILLIE   Then I hope it's the doctor . . . Is this your doctor, Marvin? If it's not your doctor, then you're going to need your lawyer.

MARVIN   It's not a doctor, Millie . . . It's a woman.

MILLIE   That was my *third* guess. You can call American Airlines and tell them to forget my luggage. I won't be needing it . . . Let me ask you a silly question, Marvin. Why doesn't she move?

MARVIN   I can explain that.

MILLIE   If you tell me you have been carrying on with a helpless paralytic, I won't buy it, Marvin. DON'T PLAY ON MY SYMPATHY!

MARVIN   She had six margaritas and a bottle of vodka. She won't wake up till tomorrow . . . Millie, I deny nothing.

MILLIE   Interesting, because I accuse you of EVERYTHING! (*She sits on the chair and starts to put on her shoes*) Is it a hooker, Marvin? Is it someone you know or is it a hooker? If it's a hooker, I'm going to divorce you. If it's someone you know, I'm going to kill you.

MARVIN   I don't know her. I never met her. She's probably a hooker, I didn't ask.

MILLIE   The humiliation . . . The humiliation of lying in bed next to a sleeping hooker and telling you I've got my period!

MARVIN   Millie, will you please give me a chance to admit my guilt? I know you're going to take everything else away from me, at least leave me my guilt.

MILLIE   You tell that hooker to give you back your pajamas, Marvin, because that's all I'm leaving you with.
(*She starts towards the phone. He blocks the way*)

MARVIN   Is that all you care about? Retribution? What about fifteen years of marriage? Weren't they good years?

MILLIE   They were *terrific* . . . but I never bothered looking on the other side of the bed.
(*She tries for the phone again*)

MARVIN   Five minutes . . . If I can't win you back in five minutes, then I'm not worth holding on to.

MILLIE   Thank God you *told* me. Can you imagine if I fell asleep and woke up with *her* in my arms?

MARVIN   I have sinned. I have transgressed. I have committed adultery.

MILLIE   In her condition, it's necrophilia! . . . Get out of my way.

MARVIN   She was awake—drunk, but awake. We were both drunk. Do you think I would do something like this *stone sober?*

MILLIE   Statements like that are *not* in the direction of winning me back . . . (*Into the phone*) Operator, get me the bell captain, please. (*To* MARVIN) And let me tell you something else: Being cruel to the Children is Number Two. *This* is Number One!

MARVIN   To *you*, Millie . . . I can understand where this is important to you. To me, it was meaningless.

MILLIE   That's a shame, Marvin. I always get so upset when you don't have a good time. (*Looks at the lifeless body*) Look how she doesn't move. No *wonder* it wasn't too much fun. Hello, I would like a taxi, please. Mrs. Michaels, Room 203. Thank you. (*Hangs up*) I'll probably get the same cab she came in.

MARVIN   Does it help you to know I didn't send for her? I never asked her to come—

MILLIE   Really? Who sent her up, room service?
   (MILLIE *goes into the living room and* MARVIN *follows*)

MARVIN   She was a gift! A surprise gift . . . Someone sent her over. I didn't even pay for it.

MILLIE   Who did?

MARVIN   What's the difference?

MILLIE *Who did?*

MARVIN It's not important.

MILLIE Your brother, Harry! He's the only one you *know* in California. My God, I heard of fancy bar mitzvahs, but this is outrageous. I bet he sent one to *all* the men . . . What do the women get, a bottle of perfume?

MARVIN I'm the only one . . . Harry's four years younger than me. When he was sixteen, I gave him a birthday present—his first woman. He's been wanting to repay me for years . . . He knows in the fifteen years we've been married I never even *looked* at another woman . . . I had dinner at his house, had a few drinks, was feeling pretty good. Harry said to me when I got back to my room he was going to have a present there for me. I never expected anything like this—I thought maybe a basket of fruit . . . Certainly I could have said no, but I didn't. She was in the room, she was attractive, she was a little tight, and she was paid for. And besides, I didn't want to insult Harry. He did it out of love . . . It's not much of an excuse. It will never happen again because not only did I not enjoy it, I don't even remember it . . . That's the story. If you want to leave me, I would understand . . . And when I kill myself, I hope *you* understand.

MILLIE (*Gets up*) I'm in shock . . . I am in total shock. I haven't even reacted to this yet. A tornado of anger will be unleashed when the full weight of lying down next to your husband's hooker really hits me. (*She goes back into the bedroom*) I mean, I'm standing here watching the woman you fornicated, sleeping in the bed *I can't get into!*

MARVIN (*Follows her back in*)   Would you like a drink, honey? I could call down for a drink. It'll calm you down.

MILLIE   I don't want to be calmed down. I want to remember this moment. Did you bring the camera? I would like to have a picture of our first trip to California . . . Just the three of us.

MARVIN   That's okay, Millie. Get it out. The quicker you get it out, the quicker you'll be rid of it.

MILLIE   No camera, Marvin? How about calling Harry and getting the official bar mitzvah photographer. The nerve of that man to send you a gift like this. What would you say she cost, Marvin? Fifty? Does she look like a fifty-dollar hooker to you?

MARVIN (*He looks at the girl in the bed*)   I don't know. I guess fifty.

MILLIE   What a cheap brother you've got. We spent a *hundred and seventy-five* on his lousy kid.

MARVIN   Millie, I've learned my lesson. I promise it's over and done with.

MILLIE   I see. And in the meantime you expect me to go to your nephew's bar mitzvah and say "Congratulations" to the man who *paid* for this woman to fiddle with my husband? You would put me through that humiliation?

MARVIN   He doesn't know that you know.

MILLIE I see. Then the joke's on *him*. Only you and *I* know that I know.

MARVIN I'll do whatever you want. Forget the bar mitzvah. If you want to leave on the next plane for Philadelphia, I'll go with you.

MILLIE (*She ponders this a long, long time*) No . . . I will not give you *or* your family that satisfaction . . . I am going to behave with more dignity than you ever dreamed of. I am going to that bar mitzvah with my head held high. I am not going to leave you, Marvin. I am not going to divorce you . . . I am going to forgive you. I am going to forget this ever happened. I am going to understand the reason *why* it happened, and I will never bring it up again as long as we live . . . I am now going into Beverly Hills and spend every cent you've got.

MARVIN Wait, Millie. Let me go with you. I'll get dressed, we'll go shopping, we'll go to the bar mitzvah, and tonight we'll move into another hotel . . . Can we do that, Millie?

MILLIE Yes, Marvin. I would like that. I would like to make a fresh start. I would like to try and rebuild our marriage on trust and faith . . . I don't want something like this ever to happen to us again, Marvin.

MARVIN It won't, Millie, I promise you that. (*He goes over to her*) I'll never do anything to hurt you again as long as I live. You're the most special woman in the world, Millie, and I love you. (*He grabs her*) I love you, Millie—

MILLIE (*Turns away*) Please! Not in front of the hooker.

MARVIN (*Nods*) It'll take me two minutes to shave. I'll be right out. Then we'll go.

MILLIE Should we leave her a note or something?

MARVIN I don't think so. She's probably used to these things . . . You're such a thoughtful woman, Millie. I love you more this minute than I've ever loved you in my life. God, I'm lucky.
(*He is about to burst into tears—he runs into the bathroom, closing the door behind him so he can sob in privacy. The phone rings.* MILLIE *picks it up*)

MILLIE (*Into the phone*) Hello? . . . Who? . . . Oh, yes. Good. Put them on. (*Calls inside*) Marvin, the kids are calling . . . Hello? . . . Hello, darling. How are you? (MILLIE *sits on the bed*) You miss me? Well, I miss you, too . . . (MILLIE *lies back on the bed*) Daddy? Daddy's all right. He didn't sleep too well last night . . . On the plane? Oh, some movie with Charles Bronson. (*The hooker's arm flops over* MILLIE. *She looks at it with revulsion*) . . . I do sound funny? . . . Well, to tell you the truth, I *am* a little upset, darling . . . The airline lost my luggage . . . (*The curtain begins to fall*) The new dress I bought for the bar mitzvah, my new shoes, everything . . . I am so upset, darling . . .
(*Her tears and the curtain fall*)

Act Two

SCENE ONE: *Visitors from London*

The living room is filled with flowers. It is about 5 P.M. in early April. The shades are open in both rooms, and the light pours through. In the living room sits SIDNEY NICHOLS *—British, in his early forties. He is in a tuxedo, and is drinking a large gin and tonic. He is reading* Daily Variety. *He glances at his watch, then looks up at the ceiling and drums on the arm of his chair with his fingers.*

DIANA NICHOLS *comes out of the bathroom, fastening her earrings.* DIANA *is English as well. She is wearing a floor-length chiffon gown, obviously very expensive. She looks at herself in the full-length mirror. There is a rather odd bunch of fabric on her left shoulder.*

DIANA Finished, Sidney. I'm dressed. I'm going to have a look. (*She examines herself in the mirror*) Sidney? Disaster! Total disaster . . . The *Titanic* in chiffon! Oh, Christ, what has the dressmaker wrought?

SIDNEY (*Looks at his watch again*) Where the hell is the car?

DIANA There's either not enough chiffon or too much of me . . . I'm listing to the left, Sidney. God, I hope it's the floor. Sidney, come in and look—and try to be gentle.

SIDNEY (*Gets up, crossing toward the bedroom*) It's after five—we should have left ten minutes ago.
    (*He stops at the doorway and looks in at her*)

DIANA Well?

SIDNEY How much was it?

DIANA Nothing. Joe Levine paid for it.

SIDNEY Then I love it.

DIANA You hate it. Damn it, I wish you didn't have such good taste. (*Keeps examining herself in the mirror*) What have they done to me, Sidney? I have a definite hump on my left shoulder. I mean, it's got to be seven hundred dollars if it's a penny, and I look like Richard the Third . . . Do you notice the hump, Sidney?

SIDNEY   Isn't that your regular hump?

DIANA   Don't joke with me. I'm going on national television.

SIDNEY   There are no humps. I see no humps at this particular time.
     (*He takes a sip of his drink*)

DIANA   It's all *bulky* on the left side. Don't you see how it bunches up?

SIDNEY   Have you taken out all the tissue paper?

DIANA   I should have worn something simple . . . My black pants suit. Why the hell didn't I wear my black pants suit?

SIDNEY   Because *I'm* wearing it.

DIANA   We shouldn't have come. I never know how to dress in this bloody country. It's so easy to dress in England. You just put on warm clothing. Why did we come, Sidney?

SIDNEY   Because it's all free, darling.

DIANA   Glenda Jackson never comes, and she's nominated every goddamned year. We could have stayed in London and waited for a phone call. Michael Caine could have accepted for me. He would be bright and witty— and no one would have seen my hump.

SIDNEY Use it, sweetheart. People will pity you for your deformity and you're sure to win.

DIANA Maybe if you put your arm on my shoulder . . . (*She places his arm around her*) Keep your arm on my shoulder at all times. If I win, we'll go up together, your arm around me, and they'll think we're still mad for each other after twelve years.

SIDNEY Oh, I thought we were. I keep forgetting.

DIANA (*Looks at him*) How many gin and tonics have you had?

SIDNEY Three gins, one tonic.

DIANA Well, catch up on your tonics. We don't want to be disgusting tonight, do we? (*She fluffs up her hair*) What's wrong with my hair? It looks like I've combed it with a towel.

SIDNEY When you played Elizabeth you looked like a wart hog and you never complained once.

DIANA That's acting, this is living. Living, I want to be beautiful . . . My hair is the strangest color. I asked for a simple rinse and that queen gave me crayons.

SIDNEY Shall I walk with my arm on your head as well?

DIANA That's not funny, Sidney. That's bizarre. You have the most bizarre sense of humor.

SIDNEY Bizarre people often do.

DIANA Oh, Christ, I hate getting dressed like this. Why am I always so much more comfortable as someone else?

I would have been perfectly happy going as Hedda Gabbler.

SIDNEY   Try Quasimodo.

DIANA   Try shutting up. What time is it?

SIDNEY   Late. We are definitely late.

DIANA   Just check me out. Do I have too much jewelry on?

SIDNEY   Jingle it—I can't tell if I don't hear it.

DIANA   Will you please be nice to me and pay me one bloody compliment? I've been getting dressed for this horseshit affair since six o'clock this morning.

SIDNEY   You look lovely. And if that doesn't do, please accept radiant.

DIANA   Why don't we watch it on televison? We could stay in bed, have champagne, make love and switch the dial if Faye Dunaway wins.
    (*The phone rings. He goes toward it*)

SIDNEY   You can do what you want, love, but I wouldn't miss this circus for the world. (*Picks up the phone*) Hello? . . . Yes, it is . . . Right. We'll be down in two minutes. Thank you.
    (*He hangs up*)

DIANA   Why do they have these things so early? No woman can look good at five o'clock in the afternoon, except possibly Tatum O'Neal.

SIDNEY   We are being reminded that nominees *must* be there at five thirty for the press.

DIANA The press! I can't *wait* to see how they explain my hump in the newspapers.

SIDNEY Oh, Diana . . .

DIANA What?

SIDNEY I was about to say you're making a mountain out of a molehill, but I didn't think it would amuse you.

DIANA Let me have a cigarette. (*She feels her stomach*) Oh, Christ, I'm going to be acidic tonight. Be sure and bring a roll of Tums.

SIDNEY And sit there in front of America with a chalky-white mouth? Have a double gin instead; it'll drown all those butterflies.
(*He gives her a cigarette, lights it, then goes to make her a drink*)

DIANA This whole thing is so bizarre. Eight years with the National Theatre, two Pinter plays, two Becketts, nine Shakespeare, three Shaws, and I finally get nominated for a nauseating little comedy.

SIDNEY That's why they call it Hollywood.
(*The phone rings. He hands her the gin. He picks up the phone*)

DIANA I'm not here. I don't care if it's the Queen Mother, I'm not here.

SIDNEY Hello? . . . Oh, yes, how are you? . . . Well, she's a bit nervous, I think . . . Do you really think she will? . . . Well, let's hope so . . . And thank you for the flowers, the wine, the suite and everything else you send up by the hour . . . One moment, Joe. (*He puts hand over the phone. To* DIANA) Joe Levine. He wants to wish you luck.

DIANA Tell him I'm in the can.

SIDNEY The man paid for this trip, he paid for this suite, and he gave you the best part you've had in five years—I am not going to tell him you are in the can.

DIANA Then I'll tell him. (*She takes the receiver*) Joe, darling, I told Sidney to tell you I was in the can . . . I didn't want to speak to you, that's why . . . Because I feel so responsible . . . I don't want to let you down to-night . . . I know how much the picture means to you, and I want so much to win this for you, Joe . . . There was no picture without you . . . Well, goddamn it, it's true. After four studios turned it down, you deserve some special perseverance award . . . You're a chubby little man and I adore you . . . If I win tonight, darling, it's not going to be an Oscar—it's going to be a Joe Levine . . . You're an angel.

(*She hangs up*)

SIDNEY That was very sweet.

DIANA Did you like it? That's going to be my speech.

SIDNEY Your acceptance speech?

DIANA All except the part that I was in the can. Naturally we both know I don't have a chance in hell, but you've got to prepare *something.* I can't just stand up there sob-bing with a humped back . . . Can I have another drink, darling? And stop worrying. I won't get *pissed* until *after* I lose.

(She takes his drink out of his hand. He starts making himself another one)

SIDNEY You have as good a chance as anyone.

DIANA I don't have the sentiment on my side. You've got to have a sentimental reason for them to vote for you. Any decent actress can give a good performance, but a *dying husband* would have insured everything . . . You wouldn't like to get something fatal for me, would you, angel?

SIDNEY You should have told me sooner. I could have come over on the *Hindenburg*.

DIANA We *are* terrible, Sidney, aren't we? God will punish us.

SIDNEY I think He already has. Drink up.
　(He drinks)

DIANA *(Drinks)* Do you know what I might do next year, Sidney?

SIDNEY I pray: anything but Ibsen.

DIANA I might quit. I might get out. Give up acting. I'm not having any more fun. It used to be such fun . . . Do you know what Larry Olivier once said to me?

SIDNEY Can you tell me in the car?

DIANA Larry said, "Acting is the finest and most noble thing you can do with your life, unless, of course, you're lucky enough to be happy." . . . Isn't that incredible, Sid?

SIDNEY It's absolutely awe-inspiring . . . unless of course, you're *un*lucky enough to be married to an actress.
   (*He starts for the door*)

DIANA I'm sorry, Sid. Was that an insensitive thing for me to say? It has nothing to do with us. I've always been unhappy. I think that's why I'm such a damned good actress . . . But that's about *all* I am.

SIDNEY Will you finish your drink? I don't want to miss the sound-editing awards.

DIANA I envy you, Sidney. You have nothing *but* talent. You cook better than I do, you write better than I do, God knows, you *dress* better than I do . . .

SIDNEY Better than *I*. "Do" is superfluous.

DIANA And you speak better than I do. Jesus, I'm glad you came. I would hate to go through this alone tonight.

SIDNEY I don't think they allow nominees to come alone. They give you Burt Reynolds or someone.

DIANA You've never liked any of this, have you? The openings, the parties, any of it.

SIDNEY I *love* the openings. I *adore* the parties. I lead a very gay life. I mean, let's be honest, angel, how many antiques dealers in London get to go to the Academy Awards?

DIANA And I think you hate that dusty little shop. You're never there when I call . . . Where do you spend your afternoons, Sidney?

SIDNEY In London? We don't have afternoons. (*Looks out the window*) I should have waited for you in front of the hotel. I could have gotten a nice tan.

DIANA You shouldn't have given it up, Sidney.

SIDNEY Acting?

DIANA Christ, you were good. You had more promise than any of us.

SIDNEY Really? I can't think what it was I promised.

DIANA You were so gentle on the stage. So unselfish, so giving. You had a sweet, gentle quality.

SIDNEY Yes. I would have made a wonderful Ophelia.

DIANA Well, as a matter of fact, you would.

SIDNEY Pity I couldn't have stayed sixteen forever. What a future I had. Juliet, Roxanne—there were no end to the roles . . .

DIANA You could go back, Sidney. You could if you wanted, you know.

SIDNEY Married to you? Oh, there'd be problems. It would be awful for both of us to be up for the same parts . . . No, no. I'm perfectly happy selling my eighteenth-century door knockers.

DIANA (*A pause*) What do you do with your afternoons, Sidney?

SIDNEY I just told you, darling. I look for knockers . . . Now can we go and get this bloody thing over with?

DIANA   First kiss me and wish me luck.

SIDNEY   (*Kisses her*)   There's your kiss. Now, turn around so I can rub your hump for luck.

DIANA   Don't be a shit, Sidney. I'm scared to death.

SIDNEY   (*Smiles at her; then warmly and affectionately*)   I wish you everything. I wish you luck, I wish you love, I wish you happiness. You're a gifted and remarkable woman. You've put up with me and my shenanigans for twelve harrowing years, and I don't know why. But I'm grateful . . . You've had half a husband and three quarters of a career. You deserve the full amount of everything . . . May the Academy of Arts and Sciences Board of Electees see the beauty, the talent and the courage that I have seen for a quarter of a lifetime . . . I hope you win the bloody Oscar . . . Fifty years from now I'll be able to sell it for a fortune.
     (*He kisses her again*)

DIANA   I love you, Sidney.

SIDNEY   Then mention me in your speech. Come on.
     (*He pulls her out as she grabs her purse*)

DIANA   Ladies and gentlemen of the Academy, I thank you for this award . . . I have a lump in my throat and a hump on my dress.
     (*They exit, closing the door behind them. Gradually day turns into night, until both rooms are in darkness*)

SCENE TWO

It is hours later—about two in the morning. The door opens and SIDNEY *turns on the light. His black tie is undone. He looks a bit under the weather. He leaves the door open and sits in a chair. About ten seconds later,* DIANA *appears. She has had quite a bit to drink and is not in a wonderful mood, to say the least. She stands in the doorway, weaving uncertainly.*

DIANA (*Peering at the number on the door*)   What the hell are you doing in here?

SIDNEY (*Looks at her*)   It's our room.

DIANA   No, it isn't. We're across the hall. Come out of there, you twit.

SIDNEY   You're blotto, darling. Go to bed.
(*He kicks off his patent leather loafers*)

DIANA   Give me the key.

SIDNEY   I just told you, *this* is our room: 203 and 204.

DIANA (*She turns and looks across the hall*)   We are in 201 and 202.

SIDNEY   If it makes you happy, go sleep in 201 and 202—you've always made friends easily.

DIANA   Ha! *You* should talk! (*She comes in and closes the door*) What time is it?

SIDNEY   (*Looks at his watch*)   Two thirty-five . . . perhaps *three* thirty-five.

DIANA (*She kicks off her shoes*)   Don't give me that "superior than thou" crap.

SIDNEY   You *are* stinking, aren't you?

DIANA   You've been gloating all evening . . . (*She falls out on the sofa*) all "pardon the expression" evening.

SIDNEY   Pardon what expression?

DIANA   "Fucking" evening.

SIDNEY   Then why didn't you say it?

DIANA   Because I'm a lady. A loser and a lady. I'm a great loser and a greater lady.

SIDNEY   Who was that girl you threw up on?

DIANA   I beg your pardon?

SIDNEY   I was asking who that attractive young girl in the Pucci muu-muu that you threw up on *was!*

DIANA   How would I know? If I were to start counting all the women in Pucci muu-muus that I throw up on, I would never have time to go shopping.

SIDNEY   Well, I think her husband was one of the heads of Universal Pictures. It is my guess that it will snow in Tahiti before you work again at Universal Pictures.

DIANA   Unless of course, there's a part that calls for throwing up on Pucci muu-muus . . . In that event, I think it's very likely I'll be considered.

SIDNEY   I hate to be clinical about this, but since you had neither lunch nor dinner, nor even a single canapé at the ball, how could you possibly find anything to throw up?

DIANA   When you have class, you can do anything.
   (*She rises and weaves*)

SIDNEY   You're not going to get "classy" all over me, are you?

DIANA   How long do you intend going on like this?

SIDNEY   Going on like what?

DIANA   Going on here in the wrong suite. I am tired. I would like to take off my hump and go to bed.

SIDNEY   I must say it was a dreary affair. Didn't you find it a dreary affair? Aside from losing and throwing up on that girl, it was a completely unmemorable evening.

DIANA   Did I tell you I saw what's-her-name in the ladies' room?

SIDNEY   Who?

DIANA   What's-her-name? The one I saw in the ladies' room.

SIDNEY   How would I possibly know?

DIANA   Oh, Christ, you know her . . . She was in the ladies' room.

SIDNEY   Can you narrow it down a bit more?

DIANA   Barbra.

SIDNEY   Streisand?

DIANA   Was in the ladies' room.

SIDNEY   Singing?

DIANA   I don't think so. There were no requests.

SIDNEY   What was she like?

DIANA   Well, in the ladies' room, we're all pretty much the same . . .

SIDNEY   I would imagine.

DIANA   She thought I should have won.

SIDNEY   Did she say that?

DIANA   No. I did. But she agreed with me.

SIDNEY   Wasn't that sweet of her.

DIANA   You never told me what award I missed when I went to the can.

SIDNEY   The best documentary short subject.

DIANA   (*Furious*)   *Damn* it! My favorite category. Who won?

SIDNEY   *The Midgets of Leipzig!* . . . a Czech-Polish Production . . . Sigmund Wednetzki, Producer; Directed by Litweil Zumbredowicz and Stefan Vlech.

DIANA   (*Looks at him*)   I *thought* they would . . . And what was the best picture?

SIDNEY   The best picture? You were there when they announced it. It came right after the best actress.

DIANA   I was in a deep depression at the time . . . What was the best bloody picture?

SIDNEY   You mean what was the best picture of the year or what did they *pick* as the best picture of the year?

DIANA   What won the award, you asshole?

SIDNEY   I am *not* an asshole. Don't you call me that.

SIDNEY   Sidney, I have just thrown up on some of the best people in Hollywood. This is no time to get sensitive. What was the best picture?

SIDNEY   I'm not telling you.

DIANA (*She sits up regally*)   I'm not *asking* you, Sidney. I'm threatening you. What was the best picture?

SIDNEY   And I said I'm not telling you.

DIANA   You're not going to tell me what the best picture was?

SIDNEY   I won't even tell you who the nominees were.

DIANA   You crud.

SIDNEY   Now I'm *definitely* not going to tell you.

DIANA   You mean were *were* going to tell me before I called you a crud?

SIDNEY   Very possibly.

DIANA   I take it back. You are not a crud.

SIDNEY   Am I still an asshole?

DIANA   Yes.

SIDNEY   Then it's back to definitely not telling.

DIANA   I'm going to our room. Give me the key.

SIDNEY   You behaved abominably tonight.

DIANA   I did not.

SIDNEY   Abominably.

DIANA   *Not!*

SIDNEY   A-bom!

DIANA   Asshole Crud!

SIDNEY   You are behaving better now than you did at the ball . . . That will give you an idea of how badly you behaved tonight.
(*He gets up*)

DIANA   Where are you going, you twit?

SIDNEY   I am going to bed. I am going to get some sleep. We have a ten A.M. plane to catch in the morning.

DIANA   Ten A.M. *is* the morning. That is redundant. You've been redundant all evening.

SIDNEY   When? When? When was I redundant?

DIANA   Turning to me and saying "I'm sorry" after they announced that other twit had won *is redundant!*

SIDNEY   First you called *me* a twit and now you call *her* a twit. Two twits in one night is redundant.

DIANA   Not when the twits are twits. *That* is being specific . . . you A.H.!

SIDNEY   Do you think I don't know what you're saying? I can spell.

DIANA   Considering that I should have won that effing award tonight, I behaved *beautifully*. I would like a drink, please.

SIDNEY You *drank* everything in California. Try Nevada.
(*He crosses to the bedroom, turning out the light in the living room and on in the bedroom*)

DIANA Well, *I* had a wonderful time. (*She follows him in*) Did you hear me? I said, *I* had a wonderful time. (*She looks around*) This looks just like *our* room.

SIDNEY (*Sits on the bed, takes off his cuff links and studs*) Have you ever seen a greater assemblage of hypocrites under one roof in all your life?

DIANA Were the hypocrites there? I missed them. Why didn't you point them out to me.
(*She crosses and looks in the mirror*)

SIDNEY Hypocritical hypocrites. They all love you and fawn over you on the way in. And if you come out a loser, it's "Too bad, darling. Give us a call when you're back in town" . . . You should have thrown up on the whole bloody lot of them.

DIANA (*Looking into the mirror*) Sidney?

SIDNEY Yes?

DIANA Was I hit by a bus? I look very much as though I've been hit by a heavy, fast-moving Greyhound bus.

SIDNEY What really infuriated me is how quickly the winners got their cars . . . How could the winners' cars be lined up so quickly outside if they didn't know beforehand who the winners were? Because it's rigged. We come six thousand miles for this bloody affair, and they park *our* car in Vancouver.

DIANA (*Still looking in the mirror*)   I've aged, Sidney . . .
I'm getting lines in my face . . . I look like a brand new
steel-belted radial tire.

SIDNEY   That little Polish twerp who won Best Foreign
Documentary got *his* car before us—splashed water on
my trousers as he drove by . . . They must have
snapped fifty photos of us going in. Coming out, a little
Mexican boy with a Brownie asked me where Liza
Minelli was.

DIANA   I'm hungry.
   (*She heads for the phone*)

SIDNEY   What are you doing?

DIANA   I'm calling room service. I want eggs Benedict.
   (*She picks up the phone*)

SIDNEY (*Taking off his jacket*)   You'll just chuck it up
again. Please have the decency to find a proper recepta-
cle this time.

DIANA   I must drop Barbra a note for agreeing with me
. . . (*Into the phone*) Hello? Eggs Benedict, please.

SIDNEY   You have to ask for room service first . . . twit.

DIANA   Room service, please. (*To Sidney*) Twit and a
half.

SIDNEY   Touché.

DIANA (*Into the phone*)   No room service? . . . Are you
sure? . . . Isn't there anyone there? I just want some

eggs Benedict . . . I could come down and make it myself . . . I see . . . Well, it's just not my night, is it?
(*She hangs up*)

SIDNEY (*Unbuttoning his shirt*) Lost again, did you?

DIANA Bitchy bitchy, darling. (*She reaches back and
tries to unzip her dress*) I found the people there singu-
larly unattractive this year. I noticed a general decline in
hair transplants and face lifts. Must be the economy,
don't you think?

SIDNEY They're not civilized out here, it's as plain as that.
Did you notice Jack Nicholson sitting there in tennis
shoes? Black patent leather tennis shoes—I've never seen
anything like it.

DIANA Really? You must have been the only one there
looking at Jack Nicholson's feet . . . By the way, who
was that adorable young actor you were chatting with
all night? Gorgeous, wasn't he? Where did you find
him?

SIDNEY He was at our table. We shared a butter plate.
(*He has started to get undressed*)

DIANA How spreadably cozy.

SIDNEY Careful, darling. You're tired and smashed. Let's
not get into shallow waters.

DIANA Oh, I *am* sorry. Let's just talk show biz . . . And
who did *you* vote for, Sidney?

SIDNEY I don't vote, dear. I am not a member of the motion picture industry. I am an antiques dealer . . . One day when you are an antique, I shall vote for you—that's a promise.

DIANA I mean, who did you vote for privately? In the deep, deep inner twit recesses of your redundant mind, who were you hoping would win?

SIDNEY In what category?

DIANA The strangest thing happened when I lost, Sidney. I actually felt your body relax . . . When Miss Big Boobs ran up there, all teary-eyed and bouncing flesh, I felt all the tension release from every part of you. What could have caused such joy, I wondered to myself. Happy that it was finally over . . . or just happy?

SIDNEY What a nasty streak you have when you drink . . . also when you eat and sit and walk.

DIANA Oh, that's perverse, Sidney. Why are you so perverse tonight? Picky, picky, picky . . . Are you unhappy because you didn't get to wear my dress?

SIDNEY If I had worn your dress, darling, it would have hung properly. Nothing personal.

DIANA There never *is* anything personal with us. Or is that getting too personal?

SIDNEY Diana, I am sincerely sorry you lost tonight. But look at it this way. It's just a little bald, naked statue.

DIANA Just like you'll be one day. (*Still struggling with*

her zipper) Would you please get this chiffon tent off me. If you help me, I'll let you sleep in it tonight.

(*He unzips her gown*)

SIDNEY   We are taking a turn for the worse, Diana . . . Let's try and stay as sweet as we were.

DIANA   Tell me . . . Did he happen to carve his phone number in the butter patty for you?

SIDNEY   Oh, go to hell.

DIANA   To hell? What's this? A direct assault? A frontal attack? That's not like you, Sidney. Wit and parry, wit and parry, that's your style.

SIDNEY   You make me sick sometimes.

DIANA   When, Sidney? *Any*time at your convenience.

SIDNEY   When you can't have what you want, you make certain everyone else around you will be equally as miserable.

DIANA   I haven't noticed any *equals* around me . . . And I'm not miserable. I'm an artist. I'm creatively unhappy.

SIDNEY   It's amazing how you can throw up verbally as well as you can nutritionally.

(*He hangs up his shirt in the closet*)

DIANA   Adam—wasn't that his name? Adam, the first man . . . not very appropriate for you, is it? . . . He did look very Californian, I thought. Sort of a ballsy Doris Day.

SIDNEY   Oh, Christ, Diana, come off it. We keep up a front for everyone else, why can't we do it for ourselves?

DIANA   You mean lie to each other that we're perfectly well-mated? A closet couple—is that what we are, Sidney?

SIDNEY   I have never hidden behind doors, but I *am* discreet.

DIANA   Discreet? You did everything but lick his artichoke.

SIDNEY   Let's please not have a discretion contest. I have heard about your lunch breaks on the set. The only thing you don't do in your dressing room is dress . . . I'm going to take some Librium. If I'm not up by nine, I've overdosed. (*He crosses into the bathroom. She gets her gown off*)

DIANA   I wouldn't like that, Sidney. What would I do without you?

SIDNEY (*From the bathroom*)   Everything, darling.

DIANA   I'm serious. Don't ever say that to me again. I will not have you dying.

SIDNEY   I'll never be far from you. I've left instructions to be cremated and left in a pewter mug near your bed . . . Ash was always a good color for me.

DIANA   Why is he coming to England?

SIDNEY   Who?

DIANA That boy. He said, "See you in London next week." What is he doing in London?

SIDNEY Acting, of course. He's making a film there . . .

DIANA What film?

SIDNEY I don't follow other people's films. I barely follow yours.

   (*He comes out of the bathroom in his pajamas*)

DIANA (*Furious, throws her dress on the floor*) Goddamn him and goddamn you! (*She kicks the dress across the room*) Goddamn the Oscars, goddamn California, goddamn everything! (SIDNEY *looks at her*)

SIDNEY What is there about this climate that brings out the religion in you?

DIANA (*Abruptly, almost with violence*) Why don't you love me?

SIDNEY What is *that* line from?

DIANA You son-of-a-bitch, answer the question. Why don't you love me?

SIDNEY It didn't sound like a question.

DIANA I am tired of paying for everything and getting nothing back in return.

SIDNEY I thought Joe Levine paid for everything.

DIANA If it wasn't for me you wouldn't have *been* here tonight to meet him in the first place so you could arrange to meet him next week in London . . . Why don't you love me any more, Sidney?

SIDNEY I've never stopped loving you . . . in my way.

DIANA Your way doesn't do me any good. I want you to love me in *my* way.

SIDNEY It's nearly three o'clock in the morning and we're both crocked. I don't think this is a good time to discuss biological discrepancies.

DIANA Faggot!

SIDNEY (*This stops him*) Oh, good. I thought you'd never ask.
    (*He starts back into the bathroom*)

DIANA (*She is sitting. Pleading*) Don't you walk away from me . . . I'm so miserable tonight, Sidney, don't do this to me.

SIDNEY (*Sincere*) I'm sorry. It hasn't been a winning evening, has it?

DIANA Screw the Oscars! Screw the Academy Awards! Screw me, Sidney . . . please.

SIDNEY (*Looks down*) Diana . . .

DIANA I'm sorry. I didn't mean that . . . I don't want to put you off your game.

SIDNEY Funny how some nights go completely downhill.

DIANA Hell of a night to feel sexy . . . You didn't happen to notice anything in my line down at the Polo Lounge?

SIDNEY I didn't take that Librium yet . . .

DIANA Don't force yourself . . . I wouldn't want you to cheat on my account.

SIDNEY   I am *always* here for you, Diana.

DIANA   My friendly filling station. Why don't you stick to your own kind, Sidney? If it's anything I hate, it's a bisexual homosexual. Or is it the other way around?

SIDNEY   It works either way.
      (*He starts back towards the bathroom*)

DIANA   *Sidney!* (*He stops*) Jesus God, Sidney, I love you so much.

SIDNEY   I know that . . .

DIANA   Why do you stay with me? What do you get from me that could possibly satisfy you?

SIDNEY   A wider circle of prospects . . . After a while, relationships with other antiques dealers seem incestuous.

DIANA   Sorry I didn't win that award tonight. Your dance card would have been filled for a year.

SIDNEY   We haven't done too badly together . . . I'm kinder to you than your average stunt man.

DIANA   You didn't answer my question before.

SIDNEY   The answer is yes. I love you more than any woman I've ever met.

DIANA   Ahh, Christ, I can't get a break.

SIDNEY   I do the best I can.

DIANA   Thank you.
      (*She reaches out her hand towards him. He goes to her and holds her hand*)

SIDNEY   You can't say we don't have fun together.

DIANA   Hell, the dinner conversations alone are worth the trouble. (*He puts his arm around her*) It's my fault for being a hopeless romantic. I keep believing all those movies I've made . . . And you do make love so sweetly.

SIDNEY   Would it help any if I made some empty promises?

DIANA   It never has . . . What's wrong with *me*, Sidney? We've been fighting this for years. Why haven't I ever left you for a hairier person?

SIDNEY   Because we like each other . . . And we are each a refuge for our disappointments out there.

DIANA   You *do* have a way of putting your finger right on the trouble spot.
    (*She lies back on the bed. He looks down at her*)

SIDNEY   Tired?

DIANA   Losing Oscars *always* does that to me.

SIDNEY   I'll get up first thing and order you eggs Benedict. (*He turns the overhead lights off*)

DIANA   You *do* take care of me, Sidney, I'll say that. And good help is so hard to find today.

SIDNEY   (*Getting into bed*) You scratch my back, I'll scratch yours.

DIANA   It's been an evening of ups and downs, hasn't it?

SIDNEY   Mmm.

DIANA   Care to continue the motion?

SIDNEY Tacky. You're getting tacky, angel.

DIANA I love you, Sidney. (SIDNEY *leans over and kisses her with warmth and tenderness*) Don't close your eyes, Sidney.

SIDNEY I always close my eyes.

DIANA Not tonight . . . Look at *me* tonight . . . Let it be *me* tonight.

(*The lights dim*)

Blackout

It is a Sunday afternoon, about four o'clock—the Fourth of July, as a matter of fact. Both rooms are bright and sunny.

The front door opens, and MORT *and* BETH HOLLENDER *enter. They are in tennis clothes, a bit sweaty.* MORT *carries two tennis rackets and a can of balls—but mostly he carries* BETH. *She has her arm around his shoulder; he has his arm around her waist. She is hobbling on one foot and in enormous pain—she has obviously injured her ankle or foot.*

MORT Easy . . . Easy, now . . .

BETH Slowly . . . Go slowly . . . Please go slowly.

MORT I'm going as slow as I can.

BETH Then go slower . . . Mort, I'm slipping!

MORT I got you.

BETH I'm slipping, I'm telling you! Put down the tennis balls—who needs used tennis balls? I got a broken foot.

MORT (*He drops the balls from his left hand, which was around her waist*) It's not broken. If it was broken, you couldn't step down on it.

BETH I *can't* step down on it. I'm telling you, it feels broken. It's *my* foot, isn't it? Put me down in here.

MORT Which chair would you like?

BETH (*Sarcastic*) The one in my bedroom at home. You want to get it for me?

MORT What are you getting upset for?

BETH Because you ask me such stupid questions. The sofa, all right? (*He heads her for the nearest chair*) Easy . . .

MORT (*Tries to ease her into the chair*)   I'm trying . . .

BETH   *Put the goddamn rackets down!*

MORT   Sorry! I'm sorry.
(*He drops the rackets, still holding her in a half standing-half sitting position*)

BETH (*She lowers herself into the chair*)   Oh, shit . . . Oh shit shit shit shit!

MORT (*Nods sympathetically*)   It really hurts, heh?

BETH   When have you heard me say shit five times?

MORT   Let me try to get a doctor.

BETH   First get me some aspirins.

MORT   How many do you want?

BETH   Forty!
(MORT *starts for the bathroom*)

MORT   The thing that kills me is that they *saw* your shoelaces were untied. That's why they kept lobbing over your head.

BETH   Look at that ankle puff up. It's the size of a grapefruit. I'll have to wear your shoes on the plane tomorrow.

MORT (*In the bathroom*)   And they just kept lobbing the ball over your head—lob lob lob, the sons-of-bitches.

BETH   When I fell, I heard something go snap. I said to myself, "Please God, let it be my brassiere."

MORT (*Comes out with water and aspirins*) That wasn't tennis out there, that was *war!* They only hit it to you when the sun was in your eyes, and they only hit it to me when my shorts were slipping down.

BETH Will you get the doctor?

MORT (*Angry and frustrated*) Who? I don't know any doctors in Los Angeles.

BETH Look in the Yellow Pages under orthopedic.

MORT On Sunday? July Fourth? You expect a doctor to make a house call on Sunday July Fourth?

BETH Mort, it's getting excruciating. If you can't get a doctor, call a druggist . . . I'll take a laundry man, a delivery boy, just get *some*body, please!

MORT (*Thumbs through the phone book with irritation*) Lob lob lob, dirty sons-of-bitches . . . (*He stops at a page, runs his finger down it*) All right, here's the orthopedics . . . Abel, Abernathy, Abromowitz, Barnard, Benson, Berkowitz . . . Pick one.

BETH None of them sound good.

MORT What do you mean, they don't *sound* good? They're just names . . . You want them to come over and audition for you?

BETH Nothing strikes me . . . Keep reading.

MORT Block, Brewster, Brunckhorst . . .

BETH No. I don't want Brunckhorst.

MORT   What's wrong with Brunckhorst?

BETH   He sounds like a horse doctor. Get me somebody with a soft name.

MORT   This is crazy. I'll call the hotel. They must know a doctor.
   (*He picks up the phone*)

BETH   Quick, cover the phone, here comes another obscenity!

MORT (*into the phone*)   Can I have the front desk, please?

BETH   Oh, *shitty shit!*

MORT   . . . No, operator. That was my wife . . . Hello? . . . This is Mr. Hollender in 203 . . . My wife just had an accident on the tennis court. She thinks her foot might be broken. Can you possibly get us a doctor? . . . Would you? . . . Oh, thank you very much. (*He hangs up*) He'll have someone call.

BETH   You should have told them what *kind* of a doctor. This is Beverly Hills. They'll probably send a psychiatrist.

MORT (*Picks up the phone again*)   Room service, please. (*To* BETH) He's not gonna get away with this. I'm gonna play him singles someday. I don't know how, but somewhere I'm gonna find a solid steel ball. And on the first serve, I'll break his back, the bastard. (*Into the phone*) Hello? . . . Yes. This is Mr. Hollender in 203 . . . I would like three buckets of ice cubes, please . . . No, no glasses, just the ice cubes.

BETH   And a Monte Cristo sandwich.

MORT   Are you serious?

BETH   I didn't break my stomach, just my foot. I'm hungry. I want a Monte Cristo sandwich.

MORT   (*Into the phone*) Hello? . . . Three buckets of ice cubes and a Monte Cristo sandwich. (*He hangs up*) Do you know what the odds must be in Las Vegas for an order like that? (*The phone rings*) Hello? (*Suddenly his tone turns icy*) Yes . . . Yes . . . How *is* she? . . . How do you *think* she is?

BETH   Who is it?

MORT   (*With his hand over the mouthpiece*)   It's them— the "Lobbers" (*Into the phone*) . . . Her foot may be broken, that's how she is . . . It's the size of a coconut . . . What can you do? (*He turns to* BETH) They want to know what they can do . . . (*Back into the phone*) I'll tell you what you can do—

BETH   Morty, don't—

MORT   I want you to go to the pro shop and buy two cans of Wilson yellow tennis balls, charge them to me, and shove them up your respective asses.
   (*He slams the receiver down*)

BETH   *Are you crazy?* Those are our best friends.

MORT   *I said I'd pay for the balls, didn't I?*

BETH   The four of us never should have taken a vacation together . . . There was trouble from the first day.

When he showed up at the airport and said he'd forgotten his credit cards, I knew we were in for it.

MORT   I will *never* travel with them again. *Eight* pieces of luggage for two skinny people? What have they got in there?

BETH   Where?

MORT   In the luggage.

BETH   Her make-up. Every new perfume that comes out, she's got it—"Babe," "Charlie," "Harold," "Milton," whatever . . . (*There is a knock on the door*) No wonder I slipped and fell—the court was covered with all her goddamn skin cream and lotion.
  (*He opens the door.* STU *and* GERT FRANKLYN *stand there. She is in a white tennis dress; he is in a yellow warm-up suit. Each carries a racket.* GERT *also has a bottle of skin lotion.* STU *has a can of tennis balls*)

GERT   My God, what happened? We thought it was just a sprain. Is it very painful? (*Goes to touch it*) Oh, my poor baby.

BETH   Don't do that! I yell shit when you do that!

STU   (*Holds up a can of balls; to* MORT)   Here! This is the can you told me to buy . . . You want me to take the balls out first? (MORT *turns away from him in anger. To* MORT) Have you called a doctor? (*No response; to* BETH) Has he called a doctor?

BETH   Yes.

STU   Is he a good man?

BETH The hotel is sending somebody.

GERT (*To* MORT) Shouldn't she have ice on that leg, Mort? (*He won't answer*) Mort? . . . Should we get some ice?

STU (*To* MORT) Gert's talking to you. What the hell's wrong with you?

MORT (*Turns, hands on hips, takes a deep breath*) I'm sorry, Stu. I'm very upset. Beth's foot may be broken— my temper got the best of me. I ordered some ice, okay?

STU I understand.

MORT It's been a rough three weeks. After a while, you start to get on each other's nerves, you know?

STU Sure.

MORT I mean, four people taking a vacation together can get very testy. You can only do it with your best friends . . . And you and Gert are our best friends. Christ, we don't have better friends than you . . . (STU *nods*) . . . because if we did—*I would have told you to shove a steel RACKET up your ass!*

GERT Oh, my God!

STU What are you, crazy? What are you blaming *us* for? It wasn't *our* fault.

MORT Lob lob lob wasn't your fault? The woman stood there defenseless with her laces open, and would you hit the ball to me? Oh, no. You hit it over a crippled woman's head.

STU   She wasn't crippled until she fell.

BETH   (*Closes her eyes in pain*)   Could you all please do this in the bedroom. I need this room to yell in . . . *Oh . . . defecation!*

STU   (*Starts towards* BETH)   Can I look at it?

MORT   (*To* STU)   You touch her foot, and they ship you back to Chicago on Air Freight.

STU   (*Backs away*)   Don't threaten me. I've taken enough crap from you these last few weeks—don't you threaten me.

MORT   Ohh, it's coming out now. Now we're all gonna hear about it, right? It started the night *we* got the room with the view in Honolulu, and you got the toilet that kept backing up . . . Only *I* didn't book the rooms, *smart ass—*

STU   Watch it, Morty, I don't like being called smart ass.

GERT   Stop it, both of you! Somebody go get a cold towel until the ice gets here. (*Neither man moves*)   Look at them. Look how they just stand there.

BETH   (*To* GERT)   You smell wonderful. What are you wearing?

GERT   It's called "After Tennis." I just bought it . . . I'll get you the towel myself.
    (*She goes into the bathroom*)

STU   That woman should be lying flat on her back with her foot up in the air. Let's get her into bed.

MORT   I don't need your goddamn advice. Don't start telling me what to do for her. (*To* BETH) Come on, honey. Let's get you flat on your back with your foot up in the air.

BETH   Let him help you, Morty, you can't do it alone.
(STU *rushes over and throws her other arm around his neck*)

STU   All right, honey, just put all your weight on us. Here we go. One-two-three . . .
(STU *and* MORT *pull in opposite directions*)

BETH   Oh, Jesus! Oh, Jesus, that hurts.

STU   Don't step down on it.

BETH   Not my leg. My *arms*. You're pulling my arms apart.

MORT   (*Yells*)   Let go of her arm, you schmuck!

STU   (*To* MORT)   It's your fault. You're going the wrong way.

MORT   You giving me directions again? Last time you gave me directions, we missed San Francisco.

BETH   Can I make a suggestion? Can we talk about all this after the amputation?

MORT   (*As they make headway towards the door*)   I got you, honey, don't worry. (*Yells out*) Where's the cold towel, for chrissakes?

STU   Don't yell at *my* wife while I'm carrying *your* wife.

GERT (*From the bathroom*)   Oh, God, no!

STU   What?

MORT   What is it? What happened?

GERT (*Coming out*)   I broke a bottle of perfume. I'm awfully sorry.
  (*They all bump into the door frame*)

BETH   My "Bal de Versailles"? My duty-free ninety-dollar "Bal de Versailles"? (*The men get in her way as all three try to get through the connecting door*) Let me through! *I'm* the important one.

MORT   Of all the stupid-ass—breaking perfume bottles.

STU   It was an accident, for chrissakes! She didn't do it on purpose.
  (*In his anger he lets* BETH *go. She grapples with the wall*)

MORT   That's right. So far we got two accidents and two not-on-purposes. And my wife's got a broken foot and a beautiful-smelling bathroom.

STU   We'll *pay* for the perfume. I owe you ninety dollars, all right?

BETH   Can we do the accounting from the bed? Just get me on the bed, please.
  (*They resume carrying her to the bed*)

GERT   Beth, be careful when you walk in the bathroom. There's broken glass on the floor.

BETH   I'm glad you told me. I was going to walk in there a lot today.

(GERT *goes back into the bathroom for the cold towel.
They are near the bed with* BETH)

MORT All right, let's get her down gently.

BETH Yes. Please do it gently.

GERT (*From inside the bathroom*) Dammit to hell! (*She
comes out holding her finger in a face towel*) Have you
got a Band-Aid? I cut my finger on the glass.

STU (*Concerned*) How did you do that?

GERT Mort, I'm sorry, I know you're busy now. Do you
have some Band-Aids and iodine?

MORT In a minute, Gert. Let's take one casualty at a time.
(GERT *goes back into the bathroom*)

STU (*At the bed; to* MORT) All right, which way are we
going to go?

MORT North by northeast. What do you mean, which
way are we gonna go?

STU Frontwards or backwards?

BETH Whichever one you do, don't surprise me. Tell me
first.

MORT Backwards. Let's put her down backwards.
(MORT *and* STU *turn around with* BETH *so that they all
have their backs to the bed*)

STU All right, when I say three, we sit on the bed. Ready,
now: One . . . two . . .

BETH Me too?

STU   Certainly you too! Who do you think we're doing it for?

MORT   (*To* STU)   That's right, yell at her. Why don't you *push* her?

STU   Can we get this over with? . . . Ready, now: One . . . two . . .
(*We suddenly hear a thud from the bathroom and* GERT *yells out*)

GERT   OH, SHIT!
(*They all freeze*)

STU   *What? What is it? What happened?*
(GERT *comes out of the bathroom staggering, holding the back of her head*)

GERT   My head . . . I banged my head on the medicine cabinet . . . I think I'm gonna pass out . . . Yes, I am
(*And so she does, falling to the floor*)

STU   Gert! GERT!

BETH   First me, then Gert! I was first!

STU   One . . . two . . . three! (*The three of them fall backwards onto the bed in their attempt to sit.* BETH *screams out in pain. Then* STU *gets up and rushes around to* GERT *on the floor as* MORT *attempts to straighten* BETH *out on the bed*)

STU   (*Picking up* GERT'S *head*)   She's out like a light! Get me a cold wet towel—hurry!
(GERT *moans, opens her eyes*)

GERT Ohhhh . . . Stu . . . Did I pass out?

STU Just for a second, hon. Where is it? Where did you hit it?

GERT I had my head down in the sink. I was trying to rush with the towel, and I stood up too quickly . . . I think it's a concussion.

STU (*Turns on* MORT) You see what you did! You got her so crazy, the woman's got a concussion.

MORT You're gonna blame *me* because your wife doesn't know how to get up from a sink?

GERT (*Feels the back of her head with her hand, then looks at it*) It's bleeding. My head is bleeding.

STU No, that's your finger. Your finger is bleeding onto your head. (*To* MORT) Will you get me a wet towel, for chrissakes!
  (MORT *rushes into the bathroom*)

BETH (*Lying flat on the bed*) She should have a doctor. Mort, give her our doctor . . . Get her Brunckhorst.

GERT (*Still flat on the floor*) I feel nauseated. I think I'm going to throw up. Help me to the bathroom.

STU I don't think so, honey. I don't think you should be moved.
  (MORT *comes out of the bathroom with two wet towels. He is limping*)

MORT (*Hands* STU *a towel*) Here! A piece of glass went through my goddamn sneakers—I hope you're satisfied.

(*He crosses to* BETH *and puts the wet towel on her ankle*) Does that hurt?

BETH   No, because it's on the wrong ankle.
  (*He changes it to the other ankle. She winces in pain*)

GERT   Help me up. The floor is cold. I feel chilly.

STU (*To* MORT)   Give me a hand. Let's put her on the bed.

GERT   I bled on the carpet. I got blood on the carpet, Stu.

STU   I'm paying for it, don't worry about it. (MORT *comes around to* GERT'*s feet*) All right, grab her feet—and don't lift until I tell you.

MORT (*Bending down to get her feet*)   Jesus, it's like Guadalcanal in here.

STU   All right, one . . . two . . . three, *lift!* (*They both lift her up and start to carry her towards the bed*) Easy, easy! All right, put her down gently.
  (*They put her down on the bed, jostling* BETH *in the process*)

MORT   Goddamnedest vacation I ever took in my life.

STU (*Angrily to* MORT, *taking out his wallet*)   All right, let's settle our accounts, I want to get outta here!

MORT   Forget it. I don't want your money. Keep your lousy money. (*He limps towards the chair*) I think it went right into the bone.

STU   I'm paying for everything, you understand? I want an itemized list: the perfume, the blood on the carpet, the tennis balls I'm shoving up my ass—*everything!* And then I want a receipt for my taxes. (*He takes out a check and starts to write*). What's today's date, bastard?

MORT   Hey, hey. Calm down. Take it easy. Let's not get our noses out of joint.

STU   You call this a vacation? I had a better vacation when I had my hernia operation . . . I'm sick of your face. I'm sick of your twelve-cent cigars. After three weeks, my clothes smell like they've been in a humidor. I'm sick of your breakfasts. I'm sick of your lightly buttered rye toast and eggs over lightly every goddamned morning. Would it kill you to have a waffle once in a while. One stinkin' little waffle for my sake?

MORT   What are you, crazy? We got two invalids in bed and you're talking about waffles?

STU   We did everything *you* wanted. *You* made all the decisions. You took *all* the pictures. I didn't get to take *one* picture with my own camera. You picked all the restaurants—nine Japanese restaurants in three weeks. I am nauseated at the sight of watching you eat tempura with your shoes off. I am bored following your wife into every chatska store on the West Coast looking for Mexican bracelets—

MORT   Hey, hey, wait a minute. Your wife bought too. What about a pair of African earrings that hang down to her navel?

STU   A year I planned for this vacation. You know what I got to show for it? Two purple Hawaiian shirts for *my* kids that *you* picked out. Even *Hawaiians* wouldn't wear them. One entire morning wasted in Honolulu while five Chinese tailors measured you for a thirty-nine-dollar Hong Kong suit that fell apart in the box. I spent half an afternoon on Fisherman's Wharf watching a near-sighted eighty-four-year-old artist sketching a charcoal portrait of you that looks like Charles Laughton. I've had enough! I want to go home! I'm a nervous wreck . . . I need a vacation.

MORT   Come on, Buddy, I'll get you a drink. How about a nice Planter's Punch?

STU   Please! Don't order another Planter's Punch. I'll go crazy if I have to watch you trying to get the cherry out with your straw. Don't do that to me, Mort.

MORT   I won't. I won't play with my cherry again, I promise. Why don't we just shake hands and forget everything?

GERT   Shake his hand, Stu. Please.
   (*Leans over on* BETH)

BETH   You're on my leg—

GERT   Sorry. I'm sorry.

MORT   (*Yells at* GERT)   Watch what you're doing, you idiot!

STU   (*Gets up, slightly crazed*)   Take that back! I want an apology. Either you apologize to my wife for calling her an idiot . . . (*Picks up tennis racket*) . . . or I'll take this tennis racket and *backhand you to death!*

MORT (*Backs away*) All right, don't threaten me . . . I got a little bit more meat on me. Never threaten somebody who's got more meat on them.

GERT He's right, Stu. Look how much meat he's got on him.

STU (*Through crazed, gritted teeth*) Apologize! I want a nice apology and I want a smile on your face. You got five seconds . . .

MORT (*Backing away around chairs*) Don't do this, Stu . . . Don't get physical with me. If you attack, I'll counterattack.

STU One . . .

BETH Don't fight! Please don't fight!

STU Two . . .

BETH Someone'll get hurt and fall on me.

STU Three . . .

MORT (*Still backing away*) I'll punch you with my fist, Stu.

STU Four . . .

MORT I'm talking about a closed hard fist, no open hands.

STU Are you going to apologize before I say five?

MORT Say it! Say it! You afraid to say it? I'll say it *for* you. Five! FIVE! I said it, all right? FIVE!

STU I'll say it *myself*, goddamn you! FIVE!
(*And* STU *lunges out at* MORT, *who is too quick and*

strong for him. MORT *grabs* STU *around the head and neck and has him in a hammerlock hold)*

MORT (*Squeezing his neck*)   Drop it! Drop the racket!

STU (*A squeaky, airless voice*)   Nemmer . . . nemmer . . .

MORT   I'll turn you blue! Tell me what shade of blue you like, light or dark?

STU (*Flailing his arms helplessly*)   . . . kill you! I'll kill you!

GERT (*Starting to get out of bed*)   Leave him alone! Please . . .

BETH (*Grabs to restrain her*)   Let them kill each other, we have to take care of ourselves . . .
    (*The two women tussle on the bed as* MORT *heads towards the living room with* STU'S *head clamped under his arm*)

MORT   You want to play? All right, let's play in the bathroom. I'll show you a nice little game in the bathroom called "Kill your friend."
    (*And the two of them scuffle into the bathroom; now they are both out of view.* GERT *and* BETH *stop struggling*)

GERT (*Crying*)   He'll kill him! I'll be on the plane with a dead husband, God help me!

BETH   I have to go to the john. Get them out of there, I have to go in!
    (*Suddenly we hear a tremendous crash, the breaking*

of glass and an awful moan. GERT *whimpers appre-
hensively . . . The bathroom door opens and* MORT
comes out staggering, holding his groin)

MORT (*Hoarsely*) He kicked me . . . Oh, God, what a
place he kicked me . . .
(*He doubles over and sits on the edge of the bed, still
holding his groin.* STU *comes out with a wet towel
over his mouth*)

STU (*Mumbles*) Get a dentist! Look up a dentist, I'm
gonna lose some teeth.

BETH Are you two through in there? I have to go in.

GERT (*To* STU) Let me see. What did he do to you?

STU It's swelling up. Jesus, my lip is blowing up like a
balloon.

BETH Ice is coming. I got enough for all of us.

MORT (*Still holding, still doubled up*) I haven't been
kicked there since I played football . . . and then I was
wearing protection.

BETH Is anyone going to help me into the bathroom?

GERT I don't believe what's going on here . . . It's like a
John Wayne movie.

STU (*Starts to cry*) Jesus . . .

MORT What are *you* crying about? If I could lift my leg,
I'd kick you in the same place.

STU (*Stands up, fists poised*) You want more? Come on.
Come on, all of youse. I'll take you *all* on!

GERT   Are you crazy? Stop it! Stop it! Everybody—JUST
STOP IT!
(GERT *falls back on the chair, and* MORT *falls on top of
her.* STU *falls on the bed, right on* BETH's *bad leg.* BETH
*pounds her fist on the bed. There is a long silence . . .
a very long silence as all four lie there quietly in pain.
Then the sobbing subsides, and we just hear them sigh
and breathe*)

MORT   What was that doctor's name? I think maybe we
should all see him.

BETH   Did he kick you hard, Mort?

MORT   Listen, where he kicked me, even *easy* would hurt.

STU (*On the floor*)   I still have a few good teeth left. I'll
bite your goddamn leg off unless you apologize to Gert
for calling her a moron.

MORT (*On the floor, facing away from him*)   I didn't call
her a moron. I called her an idiot. (*Suddenly* STU *lets out
a war cry and lunges for* MORT's *leg. He grabs it and
bites into his calf.* MORT *screams in pain*) Oh, Jesus! Oh,
God, get him off me.
(STU *holds on tenaciously*)

GERT (*Screams*)   Stu, you'll hurt yourself. He's as hard as
a rock.
(MORT *starts to pull* STU *off him*)

MORT   You crazy bastard!
(*He throws* STU *to the ground and jumps on top of
him, straddling him*)

STU (*Struggling*) Let me go! Let me up, you elephant.

MORT All right, I had enough of you, you skinny little pipsqueak. Don't you ever bite me again. You could give me a blood disease.

STU Gert, hit him! Get a lamp and hit him!

GERT (*She tries to swat* MORT *away with the towel*) Don't sit on him, please! Get off him, you fat water tank . . . Oh, I'm sorry, Beth.

BETH Listen, the truth is the truth.

MORT (*To* STU) All right. Now, nobody is leaving this room until we all make up with each other. We came here friends and we're leaving friends. Now, tell me we're friends, you bastard!
  (*He chokes him*)

GERT Make up with him, Stu. It's the only chance we have.

STU I make up . . . I surrender and make up.

MORT Not like that. Like you mean it.

STU I mean it . . . I can't breathe. You're cutting off my air.

BETH (*Lying down flat on the bed—she can't see them*) I don't understand. Why is he cutting off his hair?

MORT And tell me you had a good time on our vacation . . . *Tell me!*

STU I had a good time.

MORT   Especially the Japanese restaurants.

STU   Especially the goddamned Japanese restaurants. Let me up! My ribs are cracking.

MORT   And you want to take another vacation with us next year!

STU   Crack my ribs! Crush me! I won't say that!
(*The curtain starts to fall*)

MORT, BETH and GERT   Say it! Say it! Say it!
Curtain

About the Author

Since 1960, a Broadway season without a Neil Simon comedy or musical has been a rare one. During the 1966–67 season, *Barefoot in the Park*, *The Odd Couple*, *Sweet Charity* and *The Star-Spangled Girl* were all running simultaneously; in the 1970–71 season, Broadway theatergoers had their choice of *Plaza Suite*, *Last of the Red Hot Lovers* and *Promises, Promises*. Next came *The Prisoner of Second Avenue*, *The Sunshine Boys*, *The Good Doctor* and *God's Favorite*.

Mr. Simon began his writing career in television and has now established himself as our leading writer of comedy by creating a succession of Broadway hits. He has also written for the screen: the adaptations of *Barefoot in the Park*, *The Odd Couple* and *The Prisoner of Second Avenue*, and the original screenplays *The Out-of-Towners* and *The Heartbreak Kid*. His most recent film is *Murder by Death*.

By his own analysis, "Doc" Simon has always been "that person sitting in the corner who's observing it all" for all of his forty-eight years, an insight he explores in his introduction entitled "Portrait of the Writer as a Schizophrenic," written for the anthology of his plays published by Random House. That volume, *The Comedy of Neil Simon*, is a tribute to the brilliance of its author, as are the Tony Award he received for Best Playwright of 1965, and his selection as *Cue* magazine's Entertainer of the Year for 1972.